The Brooklyn Book of the Dead

"Michael Stephens was my Dante into dark and dangerous places that native Irish writers never knew. Mr. Stephens, sardonic, witty, places his characters in the path of an oncoming future that seems to offer little hope though you know in the end they'll prevail."
Frank McCourt, author of *Angela's Ashes*

"This beautiful, cruel book—classical in form, Celtic in language, Brooklyn-American in content—is Michael Stephens's best book and may well be a masterpiece. It's like a pit bull on a chain, and you can lose a hand if you try to pet it. Read it carefully, warily."
Russell Banks, author of *Affliction* and *Continental Drift*

"...witty, thoughtful, and absorbingly readable, as well as an important study of urban violence."
Publishers Weekly (starred review)

"Angry, funny and tender, rather than grim, Stephens is a poet of the negative, the failed, the shameful, who can match Samuel Beckett for dour comedy and Joyce for the lyric lilt. In five long chapters of increasing power, Stephens dismantles the American dream."
Kirkus Reviews (starred review)

"Lyric, urgent, stunning—Michael Stephens has written a eulogy to a time and place, East New York, and to a people—the Irish of Brooklyn who will live on in this book of the dead."
Maureen Howard, author of *Natural History*

"Lesser novelists faced with this array of characters would be content with merely depicting the decay of familial relationships. Mr. Stephens weaves them into a poem that soars. Out of remarkable bits and pieces—the interior monologues, the vivid scatological imagery, the impressionistic dialogue—there emerges a Coole *gestalt* that is far more than the sum of its sad ingredients."
New York Times Sunday Book Review

"It is a joy to read because Michael Stephens is such a superb writer, a master of language, in short, a poet. In his immaculate artistry he has given us another way of perceiving our lives and our struggle, forcing us to ask ourselves what our legacy will be."
Hubert Selby Jr., author of *Last Exit to Brooklyn*

"Even as the new debate about immigration begins to build in America, a sprinkling of books about the last huge surge of migrants has begun to appear...Now Michael Stephens has added to this antinostalgia with his wonderfully titled *The Brooklyn Book of the Dead*, which deals with the next generation, the children (the *sixteen* children) of an Irish immigrant who landed in East New York in the early part of the century...With rare exceptions, they are not the glib Irish of legend: deprived of the word *fuckn*, their exchanges would dwindle nearly to silence. But their Olympian dysfunctionality speaks volumes about the old man and the life he gave them...This is not the usual Brooklyn of distant memoir, all stickball and egg creams and the Dodgers—in fact, this may be the only Brooklyn book of the period not to even mention the Bums, and to refer only in passing to the Spaldeen ball, touchstone of most front-stoop sentimentalists...If there is a tree growing in this Brooklyn, none of this crew has noticed it, probably because they're too busy ducking punches.

"Stephens has written about the Cooles before, and perhaps he will do so again, continuing to supply a necessary if nasty corrective to one of the myths of the moment. In a strange way his grimness nearly makes this book a political statement, since so much of the new revulsion at immigration comes from a sense that this latest wave is different, harder, more foreign. Having met Inspector Coole, that seems highly unlikely."
Bill McKibben, *Hungry Mind Review*

"Although Stephens reveals much about the Cooles that is unpleasant, *The Brooklyn Book of the Dead* is very funny...Although proud, hard-drinking, shanty-Irish families such as the Cooles have long been a feature of American fiction, Stephens gives them a fresh, authentic, late-20th century voice...His verbal brilliance in recreating their gritty world brings to mind the novels of Flann O'Brien...Michael Stephens has provided an inspiring elegy for a man, a family and a way of life."
Eamonn Wall, *The Washington Post Book World*

"Not since Eugene O'Neill and James T. Farrell has a writer hurled his brilliance so passionately at an Irish American family in order to burn away all trace of false sentimentality and illuminate a core rotten with alcoholism, violence and despair. Harrowing is too gentle a word for Michael Stephens' powerful new novel: Call it excoriating, brutal, tragic. And unforgettable...Michael Stephens has made a world here as riveting and dangerous as fiction can get. His writing is as powerful, furious and real as that of any writer living today. If you're not afraid of entering hell on Earth, you must read this book."

Ephraim Paul, *Philadelphia Inquirer*

"There's a toughness to Stephens' writing; like James Joyce, he uses it as a weapon against what oppresses. But also like Joyce he can fondle a recalcitrant reality with words newly sculpted from material equal parts street talk and poetic song. And his accumulating roll of perfect sentences comes on like Samuel Beckett..."

Jerome Klinkowitz, *Chicago Tribune*

"*The Brooklyn Book of the Dead* is a stark courageous book, garrulous with old resentments and tender moments, smarting with life, painful, funny, truth-telling mythologizing, and deconstructive... Stephens takes us on a long day's journey into family dysfunction, with Joycean specificities, and the candor of a poet. So often was I brought to the precipice of wonder, laughing, and sobbing (as I'm told is appropriate conduct for such last rites as a wake), that I finished the last page in a revery that was half-besotted, and bemused with bitterness and rue."

Richard Elman, author of *Tar Beach*

"*The Brooklyn Book of the Dead* shows a master of verbal fireworks in top form. The language is rich, arresting, bursting with color and energy, as Michael Stephens chronicles the Coole family in all its misery, vice, and error, as well as its surprising moments of private and communal grace."

Lynne Sharon Schwartz, author of *Leaving Brooklyn*

"Stephens, sharp enough not to find literary 'dignity' in the dysfunctional House of Coole, does evoke a sad irony and gritty humor from the bleakness and grime of their lives. Recommended."

Library Journal

"This is dark, brutal stuff, as far from family values and the Brady Bunch as one's likely to get. But Stephens writes with a passion for the streets, for the thickness of emotion that hangs like smoke around the Cooles, and with—as much as is possible—empathy for these fractured, wandering characters."

David Cline, *Booklist*

"Once in a great while a writer emerges whose work is so different, so startling, that you just have to sit up and take notice. Michael Stephens is such a writer and his new novel, *The Brooklyn Book of the Dead*, is a masterpiece...While Stephens can turn a phrase in a distinctly Irish way and, indeed, the novel's 20 or so central characters are all members of an Irish immigrant family, this book is as American as a drive-by shooting."

Mike Hudson, *The Irish Echo*

"It is a remarkable achievement, a book of great power and beauty and heartbreak. It should be paid attention to by anybody who thinks he has anything to do with contemporary American fiction...a kind of persistent litany of woe and strife and bitter comedy. It is a book by a writer of great authority, a mature writer, in short, a very formidable artist. *The Brooklyn Book of the Dead* is a cruelly funny, wrenchingly sad, yet beautiful work of fiction."

Gilbert Sorrentino, author of *Mulligan Stew*

"Stephens' powerful and tender-hearted novel is tour de force eulogy, but it praises not just the dearly departed, but the dearly living and the toll death takes on us all."

William O'Rourke, *South Bend Tribune*

"A harrowing tale of the psychopathology of everyday life for a typical middle-class postwar Irish family. (Here are the domestic diseases that were taken to the suburbs. Here, finally, is revealed how it happened that your father neglected ever to touch you...But even here in the depths of the world of 'hungry ghosts' there is a lovely mantra I've been repeating to myself for weeks in a perfect pique of mindfulness: 'Ah, ya dirty fookin' Irish bastard ya.' Repeat after me."

Exquisite Corpse

"Choc-a-block with lively and often brutal verbal interaction, the turns of phrase alternate between Beckettian starkness and Joycean garrulousness...It is a brilliant treatise on dysfunctionalism caused by alcohol and possibly exile that will probably alienate some readers. If you can't take straight-up scenarios about violence, drug and alcohol addictions, incest and familial cruelty, stay clear. But *The Brooklyn Book of the Dead* is ultimately a devastating, powerful book, and definitely worth the read."

Irish Edition (Philadelphia)

"This tough urban novel is a labyrinthine story about a contemporary Irish-American family who live in the Brooklyn neighborhood of East New York...Just imagine a mix between the novels of Hubert Selby, Jr. and the films of Martin Scorcese. It is that fallen world that Michael Stephens captures with such skill and imagination. It artfully combines the genres of the epic novel and lyric into a new hard-boiled synthesis. This book is about memory and the past."

Alexander Laurence, *Cups*

"Stephens is an exceptional writer, always writing well, no matter how joyless his subject matter...There is real joy in doing anything well, even if it is creating variious kinds of psychological trauma, and Stephens' Coole family captures that joy, along with its attendant illnesses. By pointing out the bones at the bottom of the cliff the novel may intend to keep more of society away from the edge."

Stephen D. Gibson, *Sycamore Review*

"Great God a-mighty! *The Brooklyn Book of the Dead* is one powerful, beautifully written book. One of the absolute mysteries of art is that it can depict the ugly, the revolting, and the nauseating so that the attractiveness of the performance, and its truth, balance the grime of the subject matter. Am I on course to see both Joyce and Barthelme (The Dead Father) in this 400-horse-power prose?"

Guy Davenport

"Stephens's masterful novel is a hard-hitting, surly, and sarcastic look at the underbelly of the American dream. (He) evokes the gritty world of two generations of Irish-Americans in Brooklyn, isolated by poverty and motivated by an urgency to get out. His style is sharp and rebellious, full of attitude, humor, and a strangely hopeful despair...at once crazy and reassuring."

Harvard Review

"Stephens has no interest in the melancholy or sentimental. His strong prose is undiluted by the tears of family remorse. (He) uses the Coole family as a metaphor for family values, political correctness, the American promise and its decline."

Terry Collins, Tulsa World

"In this vividly drawn portrait, Stephens suggests that the Irish heritage itself is not only blighted but has also crossed the sea with its exiles to produce the maimed Irish-American adults of the Coole family."

Jill Brady Hamilton, Eire-Ireland

"They have returned to this always tough, but now meaner and more barren place (East New York) to drink and do dope beside their father's open coffin, their memories of the hood and what passed for their childhoods erupting between quarrels and drinks. What emerges is a lava flow of cruelties sustained and inflicted, of beatings and fights and incest and drunken squalor, of adult lives plagued in various degrees by the anger and abuse of the past, interrupted only by a few shining islands of hard-edged Brooklyn humor."

Rose Rubin Rivera, Gallery

"In the land of Menendez Brothers trials and Jackson Family debacles, few can dispute the fact that the American Family is in deep trouble, least of all, Michael Stephens, whose recent *The Brooklyn Book of the Dead* tackles the decline of not only the mother-father-brother-sister unit, but the inner city and the world, and does so at such a frenetic pace with such disturbing detail that his depiction of East New York makes South Central Los Angeles look like small potatoes. This is not a novel for everyone, and certainly not for those who want to believe that the American family is alive and well. But it should be. Devastating and honest, *The Brooklyn Book of the Dead* should be required reading for all of us, as tough as it is."

Lee Montgomery, American Book Review

Season at Coole, novel (1972, 1985)

"It's an eloquent style that calls for reading aloud, an urban Irish style perhaps, perfect for nipping out the back door, rolling garbage cans as obstacles after you, and loping over the rooftops to safety in a vacant lot."
Rolling Stone

"Don't touch this book unless you value genuine talent wherever it shows. But it can't be denied. It shows."
L. A. Times

"A host of colorful, depressing, funny, but always original characters."
Publishers Weekly

"This first novel, scarcely promoted on publication, is a modern comic masterpiece of Irish family life."
Richard Elman, *Gentleman's Quarterly*

"...a magniloquent, malignant rant, somewhere between James Joyce expatiated and Richard Pryor on a roll."
Newsday

"A bravura novel, funny and wild and language is its pole star, language that careens with a mad, sweet Irish lilt."
Kirkus Reviews

"Michael Stephens is Irish, for which I forgive him; and he has written a beautiful book, for which I thank him. It is a lyric for all seasons."
Hubert Selby Jr.

"A very beautiful novel, heartbreaking and comic, which is no easy thing to do."
Gilbert Sorrentino

"Fantastic, astonishing, powerful...shines with honesty, craft, talent and love."
Joel Oppenheimer

Also by M. G. Stephens

Kid Coole

M.G. Stephens

Spuyten Duyvil
New York City

The Brooklyn Rail serialized this novel in 2015-2016. Thank you
to its editors, especially fiction editor Donald Breckenridge.

Collages throughout the book are by the author.

Library of Congress Cataloging-in-Publication Data

Names: Stephens, Michael Gregory, author.
Title: The last thing we need / M. G. Stephens.
Description: New York City : Spuyten Duyvil, [2018]
Identifiers: LCCN 2017038934 | ISBN 9781944682927
Classification: LCC PS3569.T3855 A6 2018 | DDC 811/.6--dc23
LC record available at https://lccn.loc.gov/2017038934

I.M.O.

Linton Baldwin

Much did I rage when young,
Being by the world oppressed—W. B. Yeats

THE EARLY ROUNDS

"The mongoose then moves in for the kill, seizes the cobra under the throat and crushes its skull."
—Archie Moore

ROUND ONE

1.

He grabbed another towel and a change of clothes, plus blue and yellow running shoes, and went out of his tiny room and down the hall, entering the communal bathroom. He liked to take a shower at this hour because it was quiet and the shower stall had been cleaned by the night porter. The shower hadn't become dirty with the other tenants using it yet. He sang.

—Don't cry for me, Argentina.—

His voice was terrible, high-shrill nasal—thin and raspy.

He looked at his big, black knuckles and wondered if his hand was all right. Never punch anything without wrapping your hands, asshole. Never should get in fights outside the ring. Dumb fuck. You're gonna pay for this, man. You are going to do one-hundred-and-fifty extra sit-ups at the gym. You are going to do fifty more push-ups today. Never (never-never) do that again, man. Walking away from a fight is an action. Walking away is an action. Walking. That's an action.

He toweled off, dressed, and walked back to his room.

Kerry was gone. She left a note on his bed.

—I owe you. Thanks a million. You're a sweet guy.—

He sat on the bed, eating a banana and drinking from a container of orange juice that he took from the small refrigerator in the corner. There was a hot plate on the dresser, but he did not feel like tea or coffee. He ate a day-old roll and a small container of plain, low-fat yogurt. He took a handful of vitamins, washing them down with a bottle of cold water. Kid looked out the window and, even though it was the center of Sticks, he saw deer foraging in the backyard.

After a few moments, he fell asleep on the unmade bed.

2.

—Help me, help me, help! Fuckn help me, man!—

He was in the alley doing his warm-down, walking it off when he heard a voice. Her voice was young and scared.

Kid inched forward.

He heard her struggling against a great force.

Then he came upon them, the young girl and this big ugly guy with a bald head and a shamrock tattooed on his neck. Shamrock wore a long black leather coat, his pants off, he had the young girl pinned underneath him and spread over the hood of his Lexus sports utility vehicle.

Her jeans were on the ground, a few feet away from her, and her underpants were several feet beyond the jeans.

Shamrock must have heard Kid because he turned around.

—What the fuck, Mr. Shamrock said, turning.

As the man turned, Kid hit him squarely on the jawbone, rendering the big man momentarily senseless, but not enough to knock him out. The man spun off the girl and reeled in Kid's direction. He produced a boxcutter knife in his right hand and swept it in a big arc toward the Kid who ducked under the sweep of the man's arm. The other guy was nearly a foot taller than the tiny boxer, so Parnell Coole went under the return sweep of the boxcutter and hit the man hard on the left side of his stomach. When the boxcutter came sweeping around again, leaving the right side vulnerable, the Kid punched the guy hard on his liver.

The big man's knees buckled, and the Kid hit him on the temple. Then he threw a slashing punch across the man's eyes, opening a cut on the brow. Blood shot out of the big man's eyebrows like something in a bad movie, a red jet gushing everywhere. Momentarily blinded, he forgot to swipe the boxcutter and Kid smashed a straight right into the man's nose, shattering it across his face.

Bonebreak had a sound all its own. Break-pain soon followed, and the big man let out a horrible-wounded animal call.

Boxcutter on ground, the man fell to his knees, clutching his face in pain. If the Kid were really vicious, he'd kick the man to the ground, then stomp on him. But Kid had never cared much for such actions outside the ring.

The girl got to her feet groggily, pulling her underwear and jeans on. She found her muddy white downcoat on the ground. Kid grabbed her hand, trotting with her down the alley.

They zigzagged through streets and alleys until they got to his rooming house on the other side of Sticks, off the courthouse square and the center of town. They walked down a driveway to the back of the great white clapboard building, and entered a side door with his key, going up a flight of stairs to the back part of the house and the room that the landlord rented to him. Kid's room was small and dingy, but the girl seemed relieved to be off the street.

Once inside his room, she cried.

3.

Sticks was a mile long, going east to west, sloping down to the river. When he ran eastward, it was all uphill, but easier when he came down another alley for the westward journey toward the river. His roadwork was full of peaks and valleys until the very end of his run since he went back and forth in Sticks anywhere from four to ten times. So he ran, all alone, no people anywhere. But—

A big Rottie charged him, growling and ferocious.

Kid pulled the jumprope from around his waist, and snapped the dog on its nose with the tip of the doubled-up strand of leather rope. Usually they backed off after being snapped. But this big ugly dog retreated, then wanted to come back for more. So Kid flicked the rope onto the nose of the dog, almost the way he would flick his jab at an opponent—the way a lion trainer might snap the whip at her animals.

The dog whimpered and ran off.

Kid kept running.

—Saint Vito, Saint Vito, Saint Vito, Saint Vito, he prayed to the patron saint who protected people from animals.

After the Rotweiler, there were no more dogs to stalk him, no more pit bulls, and ghostly mutts, only skunks and possums, a stray coyote poking through garbage, even a wandering deer in the center of town, not an uncommon sight after a long winter and no food for the animals to forage.

Near State Street (that great street!), the most northern of the big streets in Sticks, he saw the last remnants of the street trade from the night before. This early in the morning a pimp and a few prostitutes, maybe even a john or two, lingered on.

A coyote ambled away at the sight of him.

Kid shadowboxed, moving sideways in his black cross-trainers.

He skipped sideways like a giant crab. His navy blue nylon workout suit rippled to the steps.

He liked the towel, something he stole from a hotel in Syracuse when he fought there a few weeks ago. He wrapped it around his neck like a pashmina scarf.

The fight in Syracuse had gone three rounds when Billy Farts told Kid:

—Put the motherfucker away—

He had that momentary problem with finding his corner. But then he made it back in time for rest and instruction, water and for them to treat his cuts and the swelling around his right eye.

Kid was six and one, all wins by knockout. The loss was a lie. A mistake. Some guy named Blue Rivers from Schenectady or Troy. It didn't matter one good shit where *fuckn* Blue Rivers came from. Kid would knock him out the next time they fought. He would not leave the decision to a bunch of bozo judges.

People were talking about him. Newspapers even had back-page articles, if not the New York City papers, then the upstate ones.

—Kid Coole Looks Good, one said.

—Coole Is Someone to Watch—

—His amateur record was spotty, but he seems more suited to the professional ranks, a natural lightweight who has no trouble making weight every fight—

—A throwback to the days when fighters fought and boxers boxed—

...six and one...

Even if the opponents were tomato cans, they all had been good fighters in their day, and they put up a good fight before being knocked out. This was how it was still done, taking a young fighter like Kid and giving him some confidence fighting professional matches no better than old-time smokers in places like Troy and Utica and Rome, building up a winning record until he was ready to go south to the Garden or Atlantic City or maybe westward into Vegas.

Even Kid knew that he was ten to fifteen fights away from a good match up—from a title shot.

So he did his early morning workout, punching and running. Then

4.

He handed her the terrycloth towel. She blew her nose in it.

—I'm Kerry.—

—Kid.—

—Thanks.—

—No problem.—

—He was going to kill me.—

—Yeah.—

—I met him in a shooting gallery on State.—

—You okay?—

—No, she said, crying again.

—Stay here, Kid said.

5.

Kid's head was shaved, and he wore a nylon gym suit, with black high-top cross-trainers, a wool watchman's cap pulled down over his ears, and big insulated mittens on his hands. There was a white terrycloth towel wrapped around his neck like a scarf. It looked as if he'd been running, only it was his morning roadwork. Running and throwing punches, doing footwork. That was long and hard work, and when he finished, he went back to sleep for a few more hours before going to his day job. Kid kept his hands high up and moving, throwing punches at imaginary opponents. He bobbed and weaved, talked to himself, then moved away sideways in his black cross-trainers, never crossing the feet. Billy Farts taught him that a long time ago. You never cross your feet in the ring. Kid ran for a few blocks through the alleys. He stopped, unleashed a five-punch combination. Moved on. Moved on up. Moved out and away…

6.

The Kid walks around the ring for fifteen seconds, bouncing from one neutral corner to another. Then he steps over to his opponent's corner.

—Get the fuck outta here! their cutman screams.

—Over here! Billy calls. Jesus, Kid, what gives?

By the time the Kid sits on the wooden stool there is only forty seconds left between rounds.

—What don't you see? Billy Faherty shouts at the Kid.

—The corner, the fighter tells him.

—Corner? Billy Farts says.

Thirty seconds remain.

Mike White, the cutman, works frantically on the opened eyebrow.

—Jesus! Billy Faherty calls out over the crowd noise.

(Boxing is a game of seconds—every second being its own eternity.)

—Jesus, Kid, what the fuck you want, an invitation on a silver platter?—

—Couldn't fuckn find you guys, the Kid shouts back.

He's wasting everyone's time now. Arguing in your corner: That's about as stupid as a fighter can get.

Blood's in one eye.

The Kid had been thumbed in the other eye even though they wore thumbless gloves.

His vision is blurry in the thumbed eye. He can't see anything from the bloody one.

—You're gonna lose this fight if you don't *fuckn* knock him out, Billy screams.

Mike White, the cutman and Billy's partner, washes the mouthpiece in the bucket of water, and then he hands it to Billy, Kid's trainer, who puts the mouthpiece back into his fighter's mouth.

—Quit pussyfootin' and knock this motherfucker out, Billy Farts says.

So the Kid goes out and does what he has to do and he gets the KO.

1.

We don't have mountains, Mike White said to the reporter. What we got is *mountainview*.

The reporter scribbled frantically, not hearing the differences that Mike White wished to articulate, just getting them onto his notepad. The writer would figure out what his interviewee meant later. Mr. White was a renowned boxing cornerman, and whatever he said was noteworthy to the journalist.

—It's chilly at this time of morning, Mike White said. Even in the late spring. Mountains are like that, though there's surprising less snow in Sticks than in Leathe across the river. Over in Leathe, you still see the mountain-cap snow. But here in Sticks, we don't have mountains to call our own. We're all valley. We're rivertown. We're *mountainview* folk. That's what we are. Sticks ain't like no other part of this here part the state of New York.

The reporter worked for the *Boxing Gazette*, a monthly magazine out of Philadelphia. He wrote quickly, having failed to bring batteries for his tape recorder, and so could not use the machine. Then he looked up from his pad and asked one of those dumb questions that dumb reporters ask.

—What are the people like in Sticks?—

—The people? Mike asked.

—What are they like?—

Mike White reflected on this dumb question as if it were a really good one.—Half us poor niggardly bastards. (He laughed deep down in his belly, Mike being a good-natured fellow.) Other half Sticks poor white. I know, I know, you thought there were no poor white people in the North. Well, come to Sticks. We even have Injuns—the kind from India and the kind from the Mohawk nation, all of them working in the button factory the late shift, midnight to eight o'clock in the morning. (He laughed again.) They make fuckn good buttons, them people. Black folk here're the old-timers in Sticks. Ancestors arrived during Civil War, the town being a pernt on the Underground Railroad. You heard of melting pot? We are one big Irish stew. A little lamb. A little carrots. Little potatoes and the like. Sticks be a big Irish stew. Only come to think of it, there ain't no Irish in the stew.

—What about Kid Coole?—

—He Irish?—

—Yeah, I think, said the reporter.

—Nah, he fight like Joe Louis, pint-sized. He the lightweight Joe Louis. Now how a man gonna be Irish and fight like Joe Louis, huh? Nah, you are (with all due respect) wrong, my friend. Kid be a mutt like everyone else here, a little bit of this, a little bit of that, maybe he got himself some Irish in the mix. Mike Tyson himself even a little bit Irish. Father a Fitzpatrick, from what I understand.—

Mike White ruminated on the topic.

—Kid fight like Joe Louis.—

—Is Kid Coole typical of the people from Sticks?—

This reporter from Philadelphia was beginning to waste Mike White's time.

—Ain't nothing typical about that boy, Mike White said. That boy almost skinny looking. But *lookn* is the operational word. He look skinny, but ain't no person (he said the word almost like the word *poison*) stronger than that little Kid Coole. He pint-sized. He a lightweight. But he fight like Joe Louis. Last time I checked the *Ring Record Book*, Joe Louis weren't no Irish fighter. He was the Brown Bomber. Nobody call him the Green Man. He was from Dee-Troit. He weren't no Irish. And Kid Coole, he the pint-sized Brown Bomber.

—One more question, sir?—

But Mike White had picked up his spit bucket and walked across the gym away from the dumb reporter from Philadelphia who worked for the *Boxing Gazettte*, a magazine that recently said that Lutrec Spears was the natural heir to the lightweight crown in boxing. Hell, Kid Coole was the only heir apparent on the horizon, Mike White thought, as he trudged to the office that he and Billy Faherty used.

2.

Kid walked purposefully across the Headless Horseman bridge from Sticks to Leathe. He had walked five or six miles in all. When he got to the Billy Faherty's gym, he was annoyed and aggrieved at his trainer for asking him to come today. His mountain-bike had a flat tire, and he needed a new inner-tube for it. The inner-tube would not come until the end of the week. So he had to walk, not having a driver's license for a car.

He stepped into the trainer's office. Billy did not invite his fighter to sit in one of the wooden office chairs. Instead Kid stood in front of Billy's desk, waiting for the pep talk. Billy Farts sat talking with his partner Mike White, the cutman. Mike was the other half of Kid's corner.

—You're good enough to get yourself killed, Billy Faherty said.

The fighters from Sticks were known for being tough enough, not good enough. Being tough enough was Billy Farts' motto. It hung over the doorway to his gym in Leathe. Tough Enough, it said. He also hung the sign over his other gym in Sticks. Same motto, different town: Tough Enough. If you were good enough to fight, it also meant that you might be good enough to die. Being tough enough was another matter. If you were tough enough, then no one was tougher than you were because there was enough toughness to keep you alive and well.

Most of the Sticks fighters worked rings in the Catskill range or up around Albany and Troy and Schenectady and along the Thruway to Syracuse and even Buffalo. Sometimes they fought in Oneonta or Cortland or Ithaca or Binghamton, too. They were all tough enough. Once they became good enough, they were just sparring partners and journeymen going nowhere.

—You're gettin' good enough to get yourself killed. You're good enough to be an opponent but not a champeen.—

The Kid sat down in a wooden chair.

—Stand up, Billy said.

The Kid stood.

—Show me your stance.—

Kid bent his knees slightly, lowering his center of gravity. He raised his hands, the left slightly extended, ready to jab. The right was cocked by his ear. He tucked his chin.

—The legs, Billy said. I don't like the way the legs are. Give me more angle.

The Kid's left toe pointed toward the old trainer. The right shot off at a right angle from the other leg.

—Closer, Billy said, squaring the breadth of his legs with the length of his shoulders.

Nothing more nor nothing less.

—Why aren't you fightin' like that? Billy Farts asked.

The Kid did not answer his trainer.

—You're losing power by turning your right foot toward the other guy.—

Billy called opponents "the other guy."

The Kid relaxed.

—Is that it? the lightweight asked.

Kid was miffed.

—Look at me, Billy Farts said. What do you see?

Kid looked at Billy.

—What do you see?—

He saw an old guy with a beat-up face. He was stocky, pot-bellied, red-faced. Billy had meaty hands. He was bald with a fringe of curly white hair.

—You, Kid said. Billy Farty. My trainer.

Kid looked the old trainer right in the eye, giving him stinkeye.

—And Mike White? Billy Faherty asked.

—What do I see?—

—Yeah, Billy said. Tell us what you see.

—Mike White, Parnell Coole said. What'ssa matta? Assistant trainer. Cutman. Cornerman. Your partner. What?

—What else?—

—Older guy with white hair. He's stocky. He has big hands. A beat-up face.—

—That's it?—

—Yeah, Kid said.

—I'm concerned that you are not seeing what's right in front of you, Kid. For instance, I'm a bleached-out white guy and Mike White is black. He's got pock-marks in his face, and I don't. His nose is big and twisted, and mine is, well, it's prettier than his.

—Says you, Mike White said.

—Says me, Billy agreed.

—You're white and he's black, Kid said. Big deal.

—Good, Billy said. At least you got the superficial shit down.

—Kid ain't Prejudice, Mike White said.

—Of course he ain't Prejudice, Billy Faherty told his partner. He's like us. He's a mutt. Mutts ain't got time for Prejudice.

Then Billy got to the point.

—You see us and you understand what we look like. I'm Billy. He's Mike. We're fat, old, bald-headed, knocked-around people. We're your cornermen. You do know what we look like?—

—Yeah, the Kid said.

Then Billy Faherty screamed.

—SO WHAT THE FUCK'S THE PROBLEM FINDN YOUR GODDAMN CORNER? YOU KNOW WHAT WE LOOK LIKE. HOW COME YOU CAN'T FIND US, KID?

—Blood in one eye, Kid said. Blur in the other.

3.

—You know what strikes me as weird, Kerry? All of it. You go out to meet your friends, and you wind up with a guy two or three times your age. No, no, shuddup, I'm talkn to youse. You meet this guy wiff a shamrock on his neck and you go to the alley to smoke, and he tries to rape you. He is rapin' you, only he never comes. No, no, I'm talkin'. You all said enuff. You all'll have your chance again later. He don't come 'cause this little baldheaded dark guy in a nylon workout suit and trainers comes along and wallops the motherfucker on the button, and the big guy wiff the shamrock tattooed on his neck falls to the ground like a sack of shit, which he is, by the way, and may he rot in hell, and he collapses from this little baldie guy's punch. Sounds implausible, you know, impossible, fantastic, made up, humbug—BULLSHIT!—

—But, but, mommy...—

—You know what they say: everything after "but" is bullshit.—

—That's what's happen.—

—And the little bald dark guy's name?—

—Kid.—

—Kid?—

—That's what he said.—

—He said his name was Kid. Where's he live?—

—By the courthouse.—

—Where?—

Kerry told her mother *where.*

—And he didn't touch youse?—

—He saved my life, mommy.—

—He didn't touch youse?—

—He didn't do nuffink.—

—Nuffink? Are you lyin'?—

—You callin' me a liar, mommy? I ain't no fuckn liar, mommy.—

—I ain't callin' you shit, girl. I'm axin' youse, are youse lyin'?—

—I'm not the liar in this family.—

—What's that supposed to mean?—

—You promised to buy me new jeans.—

—We'll go today.—

—Where?—

—The mall.—

—Route 9 don't have no good jeans, mommy.—

—We'll go to Albany. We'll drive up there in the car.—

—When?—

—Today.—

—What time?—

—Now.—

—I got to shower.—

—So go shower, and we'll drive to Albany when youse good and ready, sweetheart, love of my life, sweet Kerry.—

—You drinkin', mommy.—

—I'm bone-dry sober.—

—Then you go crazy?—

—You are all I got, honey.—

—Sometimes you don't ac' like you loves me.—

—I loves you, Porgie.—

—Don't sing that rat-shit song to me, mommy. I hates that awful shit-ass of a song.—

—Take yo' shower, girl.—

—I'm going, I'm going, don't rush me, I'm gone.—

4.

He raked the leaves into a big pile in the middle of the lawn. Then he got the large black plastic bags, and stuffed them full of the leaves. Next he found the electric trimmer and looked after the hedges, cutting and shaping, and afterward picking up the leaves and twigs and stuffing them into other black plastic yard bags. He drank some water, the sweat oozing off him like a faucet. He liked the feeling of heat and humidity, sweat and summer ahead, only this was spring, the early part of it, one of those freakishly warm days in April. He might not see this lawn again until May when all the snow melted. Or he might wait until June or July to cut it again, the cold deep in the ground, not thawing out even after the air was warm and springlike. He took the black-bin bags and put them behind the two-car garage, and then left through the yard into another one, where he did the same thing. He would pick up his money at the end of the week or the end of the month, depending on his customer. Then he paid his rent and bought some groceries. If there was any money left over, he might buy new footwear for the gym, nothing fancy, no white shoes, no red ones either. Just a nice pair of black boxing shoes, the kind that let you feel the canvas under your foot, let you use the shoe and the canvas to get your traction, to set and punch, or to hit and move away.

Fighters and alligators have trouble moving sideways, but not boxers, not Kid.

5.

—Take off that make-up.—

—You should talk.—

—I am talkn. Take dat shit off.—

—Nuffink wrong a little make-up.—

—A little, a little. But youse takn the whole fuckn lip gloss. You puttn the shit on with a trowel.—

—It's my lip gloss.—

—Not the point, honey. And cover up your tummy, and stop showing so much titty. I'm cold lookn at your bare midriff.—

—Don't look.—

—Your mouf too fresh.—

—Your butt's too big, mommy.—

—My figure's like a young thing.—

—Youse carry yourself like a young thang.—

—Like what, Kerry?—

—Youse my momma and you get up and go gallivant like you was a high-school girl.—

—Take off my fuckn make-up.—

—Make me.—

—I got the hand. I got the strength. I got a mind to. I might just. I send your ass to kingdom come and back.—

—They'll kick your ass out of this here mall, mommy.—

—I got a mind to.—

—I'll report yo ass to social services.—

—You shut up.—

—I'll tell them about the abuse and the neglect. The men and womens traipsin' in our house all hours of night. I'll get 'em to t'row yo ass in the slamma, momma.—

6.

They were in the make-up section of the department store. Gladiola wanted to light up a cigarette, but couldn't. She wanted a cuppa Joe. A shot of booze. Kerry looked in the mirror on the cosmetic's counter. Here was what she saw: Britney Spears. Here was what her momma saw: young slut out to get in trouble in Sticks. The security guard in the department store at the mall watched the two of them like a hawk. He didn't like their look. They had to be up to something. Probably they already stole it, whatever it was they wanted to steal. They stole it and it was already in their pocket. On their possession. He could get both of them down in the basement. Cross-examine them. Make them take off their clothes. Yeah. He could make them take off their clothes. But the next time he looked, they were gone, they were outta there like a bat outta hell. They were gone.

7.

—When you get your belly pierced?—

—Last week.—

—The tattoo?—

—Last month.—

—Why?—

—Why?—

—Yeah, why you do that after what I told you?—

—You got a hunnred tattoos.—

—Eight or nine.—

—Youse as tattooed as a moose.—

—Moose don't have no tattoos.—

—Youse as tattooed as a drunken sailor.—

—But I said, I said to you, Kerry, I said, what I say, Kerry, what?—

—I don't know. You tell me what you said, mommy.—

—No piercings, no tattoos. I told youse. I made that mistake. I went down that road. What I got?—

—Don't know, mommy, what you got?—

—Hep C.—

—That's from dope.—

—That's from dope, fuckn the wrong men, drinkin' too much and getting' too many fuckn tattoos. Now I got to get me on that interferon treatment.—

—Ain't you on methadone?—

—No, I ain't no methadon' junkie.—

—Youse on somfin, mommy, 'cause youse ornery like a snake.—

—Take off my make-up and buy your own.—

—This is my own fuckn make-up.—

—Don't sass me, girl.—

—This is my own make-up which I bought wiff my own money.—

—You got a mouf on youse like a truck driver.—

—You got hips like a truck driver, mommy.—

—You got a mouf like a garbage truck.—

8.

There was a way to fight. There was a way not to fight. When he fought Blue Rivers, Kid learned how not to fight. He didn't train enough. In the ring, he did not get the shit kicked out of him. He wasn't even beat up at the end of it. Sweat only danced on his forehead and chest. He did not drip with sweat. But he didn't move. He didn't jab. He tried to mix it up with Blue Rivers. Rivers turned it into a street fight, and Kid Coole was not a street fighter. He was a boxer, a prize fighter, tough as hell, but more canny when he was good, more cunning. He didn't jab; didn't move. He didn't listen to Billy Faherty in between the rounds. There was a noise in Kid's head, not words, not pictures, just a noise, and it prevented him from hearing Billy. He didn't even see Billy or Mike White when he walked back to his corner in between the rounds. His legs did not feel strong. He wobbled. He walked uncertainly, just a bit confused.

Blue Rivers.

How many times did he hear that name in his head, out walking, out running, doing roadwork, working out in a gym, at home in his bed, back in his room on Poe Street, hearing that name, seeing that face: Blue Rivers. Blue Rivers. Blue Rivers. If he said the name long enough, perhaps it would disappear. But instead it seemed to grow inside of him. His one loss. He lost to Blue Rivers, a six-round decision in Schenectady.

Blue, he said at night. Rivers.

Blue Rivers.

Then he heard another name, not of a fighter he knew or fought, just a name. It was Lutrec Spears. He was the Number One Ranked Lightweight boxer in the state, the region. People in the world of boxing expected that Lutrec Spears, not Blue Rivers or Kid Coole, would be in a fight for the championship soon enough. But who the opponent might be had not been determined.

Lutrec, Kid said as he jogged. Spears.

Lutrec Spears.

9.

—Jesus! Billy screams. Will you look at him out there, Mike White. He's doing that lost-in-space routine again.

Kid stumbles back to the corner at the bell.

Billy and Mike attend to their fighter between the rounds.

—You gotta get dirty, Billy tells Kid.

The bell rings.

Kid steps to the center of the ring and he accidentally steps on Larry Wolanski's big foot in the arena in Troy, New York.

The ref doesn't see it.

Kid didn't mean to step on the other guy's foot.

It was an accident. Like they say, it was a fuckn accident. Some corners remove padding from the gloves to make the punches more lethal. Dundee cut Clay's gloves with scissors, giving his fighter enough time to recover from a punch.

Kid follows up with a punch to Wolanski's temple. Larry slips from the punch. Ref calls it a knockdown and gives Kid's opponent Wolanski a standing eight count.

The ref makes them touch gloves in the center of the ring.

Immediately the guy lunges for Kid Coole. Being too cute, they call it. Kid knows him. He lives across the river in Leathe, but he isn't part of the regular fight crowd. Wolanski is a freelance fighter. He's Polish, a cop, and his mother is a black woman from Sticks. Kid knows his sister Tanya who is very beautiful.

After the guy lunges for Kid, they get tangled up. Kid's knee breaks against the other guy's thigh. Larry gets a cramp in his leg, buckles over, and falls to the canvas from the charlie horse. He claims a low blow. But Kid is already in the neutral corner, waiting to put the guy away now. He looks around the ring, wondering if Blue Rivers is out there watching. He would like to nod hello to Blue Rivers, let him know that they have some business to settle.

The opponent's corner is screaming to the judges to take a point away from Parnell Coole for a low blow. By calling him Parnell instead of Kid, they hope to rattle Billy and Mike's fighter. But Parnell is his given name, so why should calling him Parnell bother Kid at all?

—Come on, come on, the ref says. Either get up or have your corner throw in the towel.

Which they do.

They throw down a towel, and their fighter is disqualified.

Kid Coole wins by a technical knockout.

—I was lucky, Kid says to Mike White in his corner, swigging from a bottle of water.

—Luck favors the prepared, Mike White says.

—Consider it a fuckn gift, Billy says.

—Yeah, the fighter says, breathless.

—A fuckn unmerited gift.—

—Grace, Mike White says.

—Yeah, Billy goes. That's it.

—Grace, Mike White says again, smiling.

10.

Parnell "Kid" Coole sat in a rocker on the porch of the nursing home next to Ella Buona. The old woman rocked in her own chair, watching the trees and the mountains around them. A feint whiff of sooty grime coated the air from the cement plant next to the home. His aunt also had the feint whiff of urine about her. Urine and old age. Old age and camphor. Camphor and lavender. Ella was a ward of the state, and this home in the Hudson Valley was where they placed her. Kid held her hand and gave her a light kiss on the cheek. Her grip on his hand tightened, and he pulled away from her. He did not like when people held his hands too tightly.

Ella Buona knew this, and so she instinctively patted his hands after that unnecessary squeeze. She gave him a Mona Lisa smile, deep, loving, enigmatic.

They called her Aunt Ella. But she wasn't a relation. She lived next door to them in Brooklyn, and later on Long Island. Aunt Ella came from the Bronx. She was Italian, and she liked to joke that the Cooles didn't have an ounce of Mediterranean blood, except for Kid.

—They stole you from the guineas, she said. The rest of them are a bunch of banshees from Ireland.

—Banshee are female, he corrected her.

—Where did you hear that banshee was all broads? she asked him.

—Mom told us when we was kids, he said.

—Your mother wasn't Irish, she shot back.

—Maybe it was Dad.—

—Now there was a joker, she said.

—Banshee is female spirits.—

—Otherwise they would be banhee, right?—

—Right, he answered her.

—So, she said.

—So, he said to her.

They looked out at the countryside sloping down from the porch where they sat.

—Oh, the things in your head, Aunt Ella said, laughing.

—I don't have a fuckn thing in my head.—

—You're a sweet boy, Kid, Aunt Ella told him. You're a sweet boy, and you're a bright boy. You could go to college when you get out of that violence business.

—My mind don't work that way.—

Aunt Ella took his right hand into her two hands and held it in her lap.

—You constantly amaze me, Kid. That's why I love you. There's something always going on upstairs.—

They rocked.

The porch was filled with rockers, often filled with other older people, too, who lived in the house with Ella. But some of the regulars had died during the winter, and the new group had not yet arrived. So the porch was only filled with rockers, and no old people.

Aunt Ella knocked the knuckles of her hand against his head and said:

—There's a brain there.—

He laughed.

—Don't count on it, auntie.—

—No, no, I kid you not, Kid.—

They both laughed at that last remark.

I kid you not, Kid.

Often, Kid would take a cab from Sticks to Leathe, and then grab a bus a few towns south to visit Aunt Ella at the nursing home. When he was little, he remembered going with his aunt to visit her brother in Yonkers. Her brother had been a fighter, too. They came from the Bronx, and he knew Jake LaMotta, and her brother was going to become a ranked fighter. All he had to do was throw one fight. Lucky for him he was drafted. Unluckily, he became a prisoner of war. Instead of getting his brains handed to him for pulling his punches, he was slow-tortured and dehumanized by his captors. When he came back home, he drifted back to boxing. Then he became a caddy at a golf course on Long Island. Eventually he wound up, prematurely, in a nursing home, not unlike the one Aunt Ella lived in, although Ella Buona was an old woman and her brother had been still a young man when he entered the home. After the first home they put him in closed, Kid's family got Uncle Tony into the Firemen's Home. Her brother still lived—all these years later—in the fireman's nursing home in Sticks.

His name was Tony Buona, but his fighting name was Bushy Gilhooley, and Bushy was still rocking in his chair, even when it was not a rocking chair.

—You see my brother?—

—Yeah.—

—He all right?—

—Yeah.—

His aunt punched him in the arm.

—Whatsamatta? she asked. You can't talk to me. I got to pull everything out of ya like a dentist pulling teef?

—He's all right, Kid said.

—Good.—

What did the comic books call guys like Tony and Kid? They were ronin, masterless samurai. *Yeah...*

—Your brother knew the Raging Bull, Kid said.

—He knew them all, Aunt Ella told him. Jake. Rocky. The two Rockies. Sugar Ray. Not the Sugar Ray from today. The old one. The great one. He said he was the greatest fighter he ever saw, that other Sugar Ray. Carmen. Primo. He knew them all.

BETWEEN ROUNDS
(ONE-MINUTE IN THE CORNER)

I.

I didn't come out jabbn, didnt listen to my corner (Jesus, Billy and then Mike warnin me to keep movn), and I didnt use the angles—OK, I was artless (Billy Fartss word, always Billy Fartss words) and open for the knock/out, treatn it like a walk in the woods—and I forgot the last warnin from the referee to "protect yourself at all times," but instead I waltzt out to the middle of the ring as if it were a picnic, I never thought of it as a fight or even as blood sport, and instead wanted to give my opponent flowers and talk about how's your family, how's your corner, man?

1.

—Maybe it's not *your* fault but ours, Billy Farts said. It is *our* problem. We are your corner. It is *our* job to guide you into your own corner and onto the stool as quickly as possible. *Your* job is to fight for three minutes. *Our* job is to take care of you for the minute between the rounds. The more of the one-minute that you rest and we can work on you, the better our man fights. Am I right, Mike White?

—Right as rain, Billy Farty.—

The Kid did not follow these two older men. But he acted as if he did. He nodded his head in agreement with them.

—We need a third party in the corner, Billy Faherty said.

—Like the big-time fighters, Mike White added. We need us a full-time spit-bucket man.

That's when they told the Kid about Ralph Half-Dog, Mike White's son-in-law and landlord on Muhammad Ali Way in Sticks. Ralph was married to Penny White, Mike's daughter.

—How big's Ralphie, Mike White?—

—Big-big, Mike White answered. He four-hundred-and-seventy-five pounds maybe, and still countn. He a big mo'feck.

—That's why we got him, Kid, Billy said. You can't miss him. The next time the bell rings, and you turn to look for your corner, Ralph Half-Dog is gonna call you home. Big fuckn Ralph Half-Dog, all four-hundred-and-whatever pounds of him.

—And the opponent's gonna take notice, Mike White said. He gonna see you got a three-man corner, just like all the big-time fighters. You got Mike White, son-in-law Ralph Half-Dog, and the best trainer in the business, Billy Farty.

—T'ree's the charm, Billy Faherty agreed.

2.

—How ya doin'? Kid asked.

—How'm I doin', Kerry said.

—Yeah.—

—Why's it any of your *fuckn* business? she asked him.

—I don't know, he said. I just wanted to know. Don't you remember me from a few weeks ago?

—Where?—

—You was in trouble.—

—Me?—

—Yeah, he said. In the alleys.

—Alleys? she asked. What you suggestn?

—I don't know, he said, confused.

—Well, it's none of your fuckn business how I'm doin', okay?—

—Okay, he said.

—So fuck off, junior.—

—Okay.—

Kid slumped off.

—Fuckn guy, she said. Who the fuck he think he is axin' me how I'm doin'?

—Who he? her girlfriend asked.

—How the fuck I know who the fuck he is. Some scumbag from Sticks, I don't know. Some crackhead.—

—He acted like he knew youse.—

—He doesn't know shit, my friend.—

—Just hittn on ya.—

—Yeah, that's right, Kerry said. He was just hittn on me.

—What he want?—

—How the fuck would I know what he want?—

—Maybe he wanted a date.—

—Maybe he wanted to lick my pussy, she said.

Kerry had a way of bringing the conversation to a close.

—Yeah, that's probably it, her friend said. He probably wanted to get down with y'all.

—And I ain't inna-rested.—

—Yeah, you too cool for that dufus, man.—

—Yeah.—

—Yeah.—

3.

After sparring, Kid showered and got ready to go home. But Billy was in a talkative mood, and so the Kid stayed behind and listened.

Then Billy Farts said, sitting in his chair, feet up on the desk,

—A fighter lives and dies by the jab.—

And Kid Coole had a jab. It was like an enormous kick, like a cat-scratch, a dog-bite, like a swarm of bees stinging your face.

The trainer motioned for Kid to sit down, and he did.

—Larry Holmes had a jab like Sonny Liston's. They could knock you off your feet with their jabs. Muhammad Ali had a flick-flick deceptive jab that would make an opponent's eye swell like a balloon, then pop open like a combat wound. Joe Louis' jab was so good and hard, opponents were not able to lift their arms after ten or twelve rounds from his jab hittin' them and his jab flickerin' across their heads, faces, and bodies drove them to madness. Rocky Marciano had a great jab. Every great fighter sets up his punches behind it. You are nowhere complete as a fighter without it, and if you don't have one, eventually a good fighter who does will beat you silly. You don't take up boxing and expect to get anywhere in life if you are not willing to learn how to t'row and use the jab. If used properly, it is both offensive and defensive. Some even know how to knock out an opponent with their *fuckn* jab, rare as that may be. You keep the other guy off-balance with your jab. You puff up the other guy's face with the jab, then you slice open that puffiness with a slashing hook or a straight right. You keep him backin' up or, at least, not comin' forward to do damage. That's what they mean by 'going back on your heels.' If your jab is good, it puts the other guy back on his heels. You jab straight through their face into the back of the head, right through the brains and their thoughts and ideas, into the back part of the head, back where all their silly movies run, imagining them great fighters, receiving accolades and hosannahs. You punch straight ahead with it. Right through into the eternity of their minds. Some fighters are body snatchers, punching the body until it cries out for help and then surrenders. Others are mind-catchers. They are jabbers, pokers, spindlin' their dreams off the straightness of the jab. You punch straight forward with it, straight into the eye socket and through the brain and into the guts of who that person is. You live and you die by the jab, Kid. You live and die by it.—

Billy continued:

—You need a jab, see. You need a good jab. Your jab is the punch that sets up everything. Jab is what makes you a great fighter, not just a good one, what makes you get to the big punches, without it your game being nothing. You don't lunge with it. You shoot it out from your shoulder, stiff and straight, right toward the head. Temples fine. Maybe you get a knock-out that way. Jawbone, too. But mostly it is there to soften up the eye tissue, get the brow all puffy. Once it gets puffy, then you cut it open with the cross or the hook. You slice open that puffy face and it bleeds. You get blood all over you, but it is worth it. I once saw this guy's eye hanging out of his head on this string inside his brain. I looked inside his skull and I saw his brain. His brains were as ugly as puke, and the ref still did not stop the fight. So I had to knock him out. I knocked out the guy. But first I hit him a few more times with a stiff jab, right on that eye string hangin' out of his head. Kid, it was weird, man, tell you what, his brains were hangin' out of his eye sockets, and the ref would not stop the fight...

—The old timers say that your legs are the *first* thing to go, Billy said. The old timers say your punch is the *last* thing to go. But I think maybe it is the *mind* that is the first thing to go. The last thing to go is the *spirit*.

Billy lit a cigar, coughed, then stubbed it out.

—Have to stop that fuckn dee-scusting habit.—

4.

The bell rings.

The Kid's fighting in Rome upstate at a Knights of Columbus hall.

He fights three minutes. He jabs. Jab. Jab. Punch. Move around the ring. Jab. Jab. Jab. Punch. Punch. Get out. Move around. Round ends. The Kid turns. Confused. Where's the fuckn corner? Seconds tick off. Then the Kid sees him. Ralphie. Ralph Half-Dog, the spit-bucket man.

—Yo! Yo! Ralphie shouts. Get your fuckn ass over here, Kiddo.

Ralph Half-Dog wears bib overalls. His arms are bigger than the Kid's whole upper body. His hair is black and long and Ralph wears it in braids.

—Over here, Kid, Ralphie shouts.

The Kid trots to the corner. He sits on the wooden stool. Billy Farts removes the mouthpiece. The Kid spits into Ralph Half-Dog's bucket. Ralph's father-in-law Mike White applies an icy, steely Endswell to the swollen eyebrow.

—Beautiful, Billy Farts says.

—You okay out there tonight, Mike White says.

Ralph Half-Dog says nothing. He ain't paid to comment. He drifts away from the corner as Billy and Mike work on the Kid. His job is completed until the end of the next round when he stands and calls the Kid to their corner again.

Billy slaps the Kid's cheek lightly after putting the mouthpiece back.

—You're beautiful, sonny-boy, Billy says. You're my best fuckn fighter, Kid.

The Kid stands.

Bell rings.

Kid Coole goes back out to fight.

5.

The woman jimmied the lock to the door with a credit card that she held in her right hand and she kept her left hand on the doorknob. Sweat beaded her forehead. Unbelievable that she was doing this. But she was mad. She was mad. No, she was angry. No, she was pissed. She knew it. And she skillfully opened the door and silently moved across the room. Mad, mad. Angry, angry. Pissed, pissed. It was more like a cell than a bedroom, and he slept deeply in it. Mad. Angry. Pissed. She was. He slept like a baby. Well, get ready for a nightmare, baby.

Kid liked his sleep. When he was not working in the

plastics factory or training at the gym, he slept, ten, twelve, even fourteen hours at a time. His trainer Billy Faherty said that Kid was more cat than human. But this woman, stealing across the floor, seemed even more catlike than the sleeping Parnell Coole. And she was very angry. She was as angry as a junk-metal yard dog, pissed as an abused Rotty or a vicious pitbull. She stalked over to the bed where he slept, Sleeping Beauty and now she was the Beast, this pretty angry woman. This pissed woman. This mad woman.

Without warning, she scrambled toward the bed, then jumped on him, slapping his face hard. Whap-whap.

From a deep, peaceful sleep, Kid woke to this human torrent thrashing on top of him. He woke, eyes wide open, but not moving as she slapped him, again and again. Maybe because he could not orient himself to where he was, he simply conjectured what might be the case of where he was and how he got there. He imagined that he'd been knocked out in the ring and was coming to in his corner, his handlers slapping his face. But there was no smell of ammonia from the salts, only a vague odor of this woman's perfume.

Rule One: protect yourself at all times. But how did you protect yourself when you were knocked out?

Kid took in what was before him, a perfumed and beautiful fury of hand-slap and voice-shout, kick and grunt, curse and holler. She wore jean shorts that were cut-off near the top of her thighs and a cut-away tee shirt and sandals. Her midsection was tight and muscular, and her washboard muscles were deep tan. Her hair was in corn-rows, and her light copper skin glistened with the sweat of her exertions. Corn-rows, he thought. But then:

—Dirty fuckn motherfuckn dirty fuckn motherfuckn
bastard.—

Each word was punctuated with a hard slap to his face
or neck.

—Don't you ever never go near my daughter again. She's
only fifteen years old, you fuckn fuckn shithead.—

She hit his face and arms and chest, punctuating her
blows with her useless curses.

—I didn't do nuffink.—

Yet he didn't even know who or what this woman might
be referring to. Usually he was too tired from work and
the gym to go out with anyone. The only woman he met
recently was that one he helped in Jailbird Alley.

This woman could not mean he did anything with the
girl. What was her name? That girl: Kerry. The one who
shot him down when he said hello to her the other day.

His eyes took in the woman on top of him, slapping his
face. She looked like the girl in the alley, maybe she was her
older sister.

—Helped her in the alley, Kid said.

—What, you dirty perverted motherfuck?—

—I helped her. Didn't do nuffink to her.—

She stopped hitting even though she would not let him
up, and he told her about the incident in the alley, early in
the morning, when he was out doing his roadwork.

—Who did it?—

—Don't know.—

—Was he black?—

—What's it matter?—

—It matters.—

—Are you black?—

—What the fuck is it to you?—

She was the color of half the people in Sticks, give or take a black father or a Bangladeshi mother, one parent Spanish-speaking, the other American Indian.

—He was your color, Kid said. Whatever you are, he was that color.

—What you mean by that, I'm axing you? You Prejudice?—

—I ain't no Prejudice, he said. I'm a mutt too.

—Mutt, my fuckn ass.—

—You gonna let me up?—

—So was he black?—

—He was like you.—

—I'm black, she said.

He sat up.

—Can I pee?—

—Not so fast, she said.

She pulled the sheet off him. Pulled down his pants. She slid out of her cut-away jean shorts. She hopped on the piss erection. But he could not come because of the piss he needed to let go of, so after awhile, she stopped.

—Go to the baretroom.—

—Thanks, he said, stepping over her.

He went down the hall and looked in the mirror. His face was red on one side from her hitting it. The welt resembled his face when he'd been fighting, not covering up, and the stinging end of a jab swelled up the skin under his eyes.

He put cold water on his face, and it felt good. Then he went back to the room, imagining a brilliant rendezvous with this destructive angel. He imagined resuming what they left off, only now he was ready to go to town with her. Ready, ready, to rock 'n' roll. Ready to boogie. He was ready to rumble. Let's get ready to...

When he walked in the door, the woman was gone. No note, no signs, just a hollow space where she had been, an empty space and the silence.

—Damn, he said, wishing that he had not gotten out of bed so quickly, that he did not have a piss-erection, but the real deal to do her good, because she was a fox, man, she was looking good. She was a looker, man. The girl be lookin' tight, she be fine, man. She had style, a high-class ass and high cheekbones. Damn, she had corn-rows. He loved them corn-rows, all lined up in a row, like, like corn. Yeah.

She was like sweet corn. Only now she's gone.

What a shame, man.

So he got up and went into his gear, put on his running shoes, and went out the door to do his roadwork.

He ran up and down the alleys, back and forth, time and again, east to west, west to east, hardly breaking a sweat, praying he didn't run into any vicious dogs. He also prayed that he would see her again.

What did she say her name was?

His punches sailed through the air at imaginary targets, at imagined opponents. He threw combinations, though holding back just a little. If he were to throw punches at full-force, he'd pull a muscle in his back. You needed an object to land on if you weren't going to pull a muscle. You needed a face or a stomach, a liver or a spleen, the chest or the Adam's apple. You punched through the object to the other side. But shadow-boxing, you held back. You didn't want to pull a muscle doing roadwork. That would be what Billy Faherty called

—*counterproductive*—

What was her name?

Her name was: what?

Peaches. Nah. Candy. Nah. Tiffany or Dawn. Nah.

Cornrows in a row, like, like, like corn.

Like corn, man.

ROUND FOUR

1.

In the Kid's corner Billy Faherty screams. The cutman Mike White talks. The spit-bucketman Ralph Half-Dog adds his two cents. Everyone yaps all at once so Kid can't hear any of them.

—Quit chimin' in, his trainer Billy says. Shuddafuckup!

Everyone gets quiet. Billy Faherty is boss.

—*Shut up*! he says. Shuddafuckup! Let him rest. Don't confuse him. Let the Kid get his bearings. Let me do the talkn.

Billy squats down in front of his fighter.

—Don't stand there, Kid. Move. If he's hittn, get on your bicycle, and ride. If you get an angle, take it. Take the advantage. For god's sake, son, protect yourself. You may not give a shit that you're gettn hit, but I give a shit about you gettn hit. It hurts me to see you hit like that. You're like the son I never had, Kid.

(Mike White would later remind Billy Farts that he had eleven children, many of them boys.)

Billy's voice comes through the noise of the crowd.

—Quit chimin' in, you morons, he says to the other cornermen in the heated, sweaty intensity of the fight card.

He holds the fighter's face in his hands. Then he looks the Kid in the eyes. He has the young man's attention as the fighter sits on the stool, getting his wind and energy

67

back. Kid's heartbeat goes from 180 beats-per-minute back to 45 in one minute flat. The Kid drinks the water from the sponge, soaking it into every part of his thirsty body.

—He's ahead, Billy says. You can't win on fuckn pints.

The Kid wants to ask him

—What do I do?—

But the fighter has no words.

Billy understands, having been there. He had been down in points like Kid Coole was.

—Knock him out, Billy Farts says.

He whispers it in the fighter's ear.

—Knock him out. Knock the motherfucker out.—

Billy Faherty whispers these words in Kid's ear the way a lover might whisper I love you.

—Knock out this fuck.—

So the Kid does. He did. He knocks out the other guy. Now he's ten and one.

2.

In the aftermath of the fight, driving back to Sticks, Mike White reminded Billy Faherty that he had eleven children. What's the pint? Billy asked. The pernt was that Billy had told Kid that he was like the son Billy never had. Billy Farts laughed. Don't take me literally, he told his friend Mike White. Why did you say that then? Mike asked.

—A figure of speech, Billy Farts said.

—Billy's what they call a psychologist, Mike White said

to his son-in-law, Ralph Half-Dog. He understands human nature, human beings and how they behave.

Ralph ate a burrito, and could care less about psychology, although he had enjoyed working the corner with his father-in-law, Mike White.

—See, Mike White explained to big Ralph, In the ring, Kid can't remember the fact that Billy had eleven children. In fact, there are no facts on his mind, nothing like a fact in his head. All he can remember, goin' back into the center of the ring, is the last thing Billy says to him, that he cares about the Kid even if the Kid didn't care about himself, which is true enough. Billy thinks highly of Kid Coole as a boxer, but also as a human being. He thinks the world of him. He likes the Kid's quiet nature, his clean-cut manner, the way he don't get into trouble. He don't make trouble that boy.

—Plus, he's a fuckn good fighter, Ralph said.

Ralph, as usual, wore bib overalls, with a long black ponytail, being Iroquois, people who didn't believe in chopping off their hair, which was sacred to them.

—Plus that, son. Even if Kid could not listen to anyone else in his corner, he could hear Billy. Sometimes it's hard to get through a fighter's thick skull. No, not sometimes, it's always hard to get through to fighters. They've got defenses. Walls all around them. Problems with communication with others. They're all loners. But he likes Billy and me and now you, Ralph. Plus Kid's not as thick as the others. He's what you'd call flexible.—

—Malleable, Ralph said, remembering Billy saying it earlier.

—Uh huh, Mike White replied. He's malleable. He'll listen to you. He knows how to readjust his fight after Billy give him instructions.

—Jab, jab, jab, Ralph Half-Dog said.

The spit-bucket man.

—Combinations, Mike White the cutman said, not contradicting his son-in-law so much as verbally counterpunching him.

You could listen to Mike White's advice. The only trouble was that you couldn't hear him because of the noise around the arena. Even if Kid wanted to listen to Mike White's advice, the fighter couldn't hear him.

Billy Faherty was another story altogether. He had a big, thick Irish brogued-Brooklyn accent. His words came through. His voice was so loud because he grew up in a saloon and he had to call sandwich orders into the kitchen from his father behind the bar to his mother in the back, and he had to do it over a roomful of working men drinking, a jukebox, the TV blaring.

3.

Gladiola lived on the other side of the courthouse square. Down Mountain Avenue. Before the Little League ball field and the button factory. Her house was big and crumbling, big and run-down; it had once been grand and now was falling apart. The living and dining rooms looked all right, but they had a foul damp odor to them. The kitchen was so old, it was a joke. She had a sink that looked like a basin you'd find in a gas station. The stove was fired by wood. Her refrigerator had a condenser on top, probably from the 1950s or earlier, and this was the 21st century.

There was an oil cloth on the table and it was streaked with peanut butter and jelly, sticky and dirty both. None of the chairs matched. None of the plates matched. The silverware came from diners where she stole it, piece by piece. The glasses were jelly jars. The linen was paper towels. The place mats she got from a fast-food joint on Route 9. There was a bare light-bulb over the dining room table. Paint chipped from the walls. Wallpaper peeled off another wall. The floorboards were wide, with big gaping holes in between the boards; they needed sanding, and had food stains and animal fur on them.

Upstairs, it was worse, the plaster had fallen off the ceiling and the walls, showing the old wooden lats and the guts of the building. The attic had no floor and the roof leaked. They tended to do everything, including their sleep, on the ground floor. Kerry slept in a room off the kitchen. Gladiola slept in a small room off the living room. In the old days, it was called the birthing room, because that was where people were born.

Kerry was born there, too, with a midwife assisting the teenage mother.

Before coming to Sticks, Gladiola lived in the Bronx. Her father was a fireman. She had eight brothers and sisters. They lived on City Island. Although she told everyone that her family was Irish and Shinnecock Indian from out on the end of Long Island, her mother was from Jamaica, both the island in the Caribbean and later the neighborhood in Queens. Her father was Irish, Italian, and probably Mohawk. That's what she told Kid as he sat there in her big, messy kitchen.

—It was a nice life, she said.

But she was not convincing, and he didn't believe her anyhow. Kid didn't know anyone who had a nice life.

—We never wanted for anything material, Kid. We just didn't get much love from my parents. They were as needy as their children.

Kid had run into her in the Price Chopper out by Route 9, and he turned on his heels when he saw her looking at him in the ice cream aisle. She ran after him, told him to wait, she apologized, said she was being crazy. Would he come by her house? She believed him. So he was sitting there in that ramshackle big house on the other side of the court-house square. Gladiola was in storytelling mode, and Kid was the perfect audience, being someone who rarely spoke, much less told stories.

—I got pregnant. Fifteen years old. Jeez. Parents would not let me have an abortion. They planned to give up the baby for adoption once it was born. There was no question of me marrying or keeping the baby. So I left home. Moved to Sticks. I knew a guy who had done time in the prison and I'd visited him with a friend who went out with the guy. It was far enough away and far enough from the Bronx for them not to find me if they even bothered to look. Probably they didn't look.

—Sticks was a town of outcasts. No one blinked when I entered. Rented a room upstairs in this very house. Eventually I had a boyfriend who, with his drug-money earnings, purchased the house for a few thousand dollars. When I was eighteen, he put the house in both our names, even though we were not married. Then he o.d.ed in the bathroom off the kitchen. The house became mine.

—I was eighteen years old, a mother of a three-year-old child, jobless, penniless, but I had me a big-ass house in Sticks. So I took in boarders. Fixed it up. This is as far as I've got on my fix-up project. Fifteen years, man. The downstairs rooms are inhabitable, but only barely. Some days the moldy, mildewed smells overwhelm the best of us. But it was better than when Jocko Reiss owned it with me. He could fix anything, Jocko, only he had a bad jones for smack.—

Kid noticed that her street manner, her slangy way of talking, had gone away, and she spoke in a normal voice, not edgy, not tough, not from the 'hood. He liked it. Kid didn't go for the street talk, the street jive, the street attitude. Fuck that street attitude, he thought. I want to be as clean-cut and simple-living as I can be. I want to be a model for people. I want to be what Billy Farts told me to be—dignified. A man of dignity and worth. Yeah, I want to be dignified and outstanding.

But Gladiola was back to talking to him again.

—People used to rent the upstairs rooms. But most of them were doing crack, and they were the ones who stripped the ceilings and the walls. They were the ones who stole the original fixtures to sell them to the antique dealers on Harding Avenue. Sticks was a bit of an antiques capital even then. But only Harding Avenue, just like now. The rest of the town is still the same, never changing, keeping its old veneer, its odors. Hey, man, did you know that this town was a whorehouse for sailors in the 19th century, a whorehouse for bootleggers and then drug dealers in the 20th. In the 21st century, very little's changed, you ax me. Now Sticks is a crackhouse for the Hudson Valley, a place where state workers from Albany can find cheap whores and even cheaper drugs, and it's far enough from the capital not to cause them any trouble. Likewise, the other direction: it's far enough from New York City, so that if you're fleeing a life down there, no one bothers to come this far to find you.

—The newcomers are all people from the City, artists and the like. The antique dealers. Two-home people from the northern suburbs. Me, I'm part of the old guard. Every once in a while, a painter might ask me to pose for him or her, and I will, but mostly I stick with the others, the you know outsiders, people like you and me, I don't mix with the newcomers, the people from the city, the artsy-fartsy crowd. Give me the flat-foot waitresses from the diners on Route 9. Give me the beer-bellied motorcyclists from the riverfront. I like people who are tattooed and pierced, wandering the streets looking for drugs or a glass of whiskey. If Sticks had a Mary Magdalene, I'm it. I'm her. Gladiola Magdalene.

5.

—What's your story, Kid? How did you wind up here?—

—Mr. Patterson, he said.

—Patterson, who he, a social worker?—

—A boxer, Kid said.

6.

Kid didn't drink, didn't smoke, stay up late, or curse much. He barely talked. He was like a ghost, she thought, so quiet and stalking around the edges of rooms. He was so dark and quiet. He was so still. He was like a monk. He had got that, what? Yeah, serenity. He had gotten a tranquility about him. He was peaceful. When you shook his hand, you expected he'd do it hard. But he was soft, his handshake was as loose as a girl's. If you squeezed his hand, he pulled away. He was shy, Gladiola thought.

—She's too young to fuck, she said to him.

—Who?—

—Don't play fuckn dumb with me, Kid. You know who I mean. My daughter. She's only fifteen. Don't fuck around with her. Friends, okay. But don't fuck around. That's a warning, man.—

—I'm cool, he said.

—You cool all right, Gladiola answered back. You Kid Coole, that's who you is. You fuckn Kid Coole. You could be a fuckn rapper with that name. You could be a gang-banger.

You could be hip-hopping down Harlem and Bed-Stuy with a moniker like that. You could be the king pimp on State Street with that johnson.

—I saved her life, he said, matter-of-factly.

—That's why I let youse in my house. But don't get no ideas from being here that you can get cozy with her. Not with me neither. I don't even like men. Women is a lot prettier than men.—

—I like you, he said.

—Well, I don't like you, man.—

7.

—If the cut opens up, Billy says, I'm gonna stop the fight.

The cut is a bad one, in a bad spot. On the eyelid. Top part. A good punch would open it. A jab opens the cut. The blood rolls off the eyelid into his right eye. It is warm and it blinds him. He can't see the other guy's left hooks and that jab he stings Kid Coole with. He hates it, that jab. It is a nasty punch. At first, it did not seem like anything. But as the opponent kept landing the jab, it stung, then it began to hurt. He cannot explain the feeling he had when the eyelid opened. How was there even time for explanations? Kid could feel the eye dangling in its socket. The last thing in the world Kid wants is for someone to punch it.

He is blind in one eye and he can't see from that side. But he times it. He counts. One-two-three. Jab. One-two. Double jab. Kid takes the first jab. Counts. As the other guy lets go of the first part of the double jab, Kid slips under the jab, and he whacks the opponent good on the ribs. It feels good to be so close to him, hearing his breath. Kid knows the guy can't jab from the inside. He follows the rib shot with an uppercut, and it lands on the guy's lower jaw. He can almost feel the other guy's feet leaving the canvas, and the body becoming weightless. It is the fifth round, right toward the end of it. Kid comes over the top with a right cross. Then he hits his opponent on the liver with a left hook. Kid hits him in the heart, and the other guy is out on his feet. But the other guy won't go down.

Another uppercut.

A left to the head.

A right to the head.

The opponent grabs Kid and holds on. Don't get cute with me now. Don't try to dance with me until the bell rings, and then dance your way through the last round and a win.

Kid's blood runs down his opponent's back. Kid doesn't even know if he has an eye left. The adrenaline runs through him so fast he knows he won't be able to answer the bell for the final round if he does not put the other guy away now. The other guy has Kid tied up. If the ref breaks the clinch, Kid believes that the guy will fall on his face.

The ref shouts:

—Punch out of the clinch—

But the referee does not separate them.

Kid bucks and jiggles and does everything to break the guy's grip, and just when Kid is ready to give up, the opponent lets go.

His hands are at his sides. He has eyes that are like Christ's on the cross. The eyes are turned heavenward. They're filled with piety.

There is no more fight in this guy. He looks like an angel about to ascend into Heaven.

Kid throws a left to the body. He throws a right. The other guy's glove catches it because he now tries to cover up, to protect himself. That's when Kid Coole lands a big straight right on the temple.

The opponent falls like a sack of potatoes. He goes down like a sack of shit on the canvas.

The referee counts him out.

Kid's twelve and one now.

8.

Kid came by the gym in Sticks, a butterfly stitch in his eyebrow and down through the socket of his eye. He sat in the office waiting to talk with Billy Farts who was on the telephone trying to *affect* a fight for Kid Coole. Billy's eyebrows were filled with scar tissue, too. His hands were criss-crossed with scars. Kid once saw Billy with his shirt off, and he had a long scar from sternum to belly. He'd had open-heart surgery, plus part of his stomach removed.

When Billy Farts got off the telephone, it was almost like he was reading Kid's mind about the scars. Billy Farts had a far-away look, dreamy and nostalgic. He said:

—It's in the genes. Some fighters bleed. Others don't cut easy. They're *resilient*—

—Resilient, Mike White said. What the fuck, man. Billy's got himself some *vocabulary*, hey, Kiddo? His head filled with all kindsa shee-it. Now I thought resilient was something good raincoats had. I didn't know it was a thing a great fighter had.

Then Billy Farts said,

—They have the ability to recover quickly from misfortune. I never met a raincoat that suffered from misfortune—

—That's 'cause you never watched Colombo on the television, Mike said.

Resilient. Something good raincoats had. Like Colombo's. They recovered easily from misfortune, like being wet and crumbled in the bottom of the hall closet. English raincoats were resilient. They had silicone *impregnated* in them, Mike White thought. Kid Coole was like a good English raincoat. Punches popped right off him like rain beading down off a good raincoat made in England. That's about all England was good for, as far as Mike White could tell. They weren't that good with their boxers, except for one or two, that Lennox heavyweight, and that light-heavy from Wales, the one with the Italian name. Joe Calzaghe. But Wales ain't England, Billy Farts once told Mike White. Wales was Keltic, just like Ireland and Scotland. Maybe you had to be Keltic to be truly resilient.

—White fighters cut easier than us black folk, Mike White said.

—Says who?—

—Says me, Mike said.

—Bullshit, Billy Farts said. Bull-fuckn-shit.

—Truth, Mike White answered back.

—Truth, my ass, Billy said. Resilient fighters do not cut, be they black or white. I seen black guys cut and bleed just as bad as the lily-white Irish fighters of my yout'. I seen white guys like Billy Conn not cut and bleed. Go figure, huh?

—They were waterproof, Mike said. They was like the stuff on raincoats. Resilient.

—God had to give you something good, Billy said to his partner and friend. The Higher Power gave you something good because of all the shit He gave you. But pain is the touchstone of spirituality.

—Praise the Lord, Mike White shouted. God is good, Billy. God is great, Billy Farty. And I think the Kid's okay.—

—Pain is the touchstone, Billy Farts repeated.

9.

Mike White was a road-map of scars. Besides the scars in his eyebrows and under his eyes and across the bridge of his nose, he had scars on his face that have nothing to do with boxing. Some kind of pox he had as a child. His skin was so dark, you couldn't see the scars unless he was close up. And he had a long scar down a cheek.

There were open-heart surgical scars on Mike White, too. Plus his body was filled with knife, broken bottle, and bullet scars.

—Black America ain't always Dream City, Mike White said. You cut or be cut. I cut me some, and some cut me. Eye for eye, Kid, just like the Lord say. Safest place for me's the gym. I feel right at home in the ring, then I got comfortable in the corner. The corner's home to me. I feel safe there. It's my bunker.

—Don't listen to his shit, Billy Faherty shouted. Mike White was born ugly. He makes Sonny Liston look handsome.

Then Billy got serious. He looked over at the Kid.

—You keep cutting like that, Billy said, you won't have too many more fights left in you. Believe me, sonny boy. You cut like that, and it's over. Lucky for you Mike White's your cutman. Mike knows a thing or two about stanchn a wound. Am I right, Mike White?

—Right as rain, Billy.—

—You cut like that, Billy Faherty said, you ain't gonna be able to sustain an effective defense against the jab. You're not gonna be in this business much longer, mister.

Mike White defended Kid and said the Kid had strong skin.

—He's like Ali, Mike said. The Kid don't cut easy. That was a motherfuckn headbutt. Kid don't cut.

—Yeah, that was way back when, Billy said. But now he cuts. He cuts all right because he's all cut up, Mike White. It don't matter a fuck whether it was headbutt or straight right. A cut's a *fuckn* cut. He got opened up, and that means in the future, he's more likely to open again, right at the fuckn pint where the last fuckn event took place. Right on his fuckn eye, Mike.

10.

Kid Coole had scars in his eyebrows and over his eyelid now. He had scars on his cheekbones and on the bridge of his nose. But he had more breaks than scars. His nose had been broken so many times that he had lost count. But instead of looking at what he did not have, Kid tried to focus on what he did have. He had his legs. He had his balance. A good punch. His spirit was good. He was focused. He knew how to concentrate. He was in great shape. He didn't drink or smoke or take drugs or hang out or do weird things that hurt his body. He didn't eat meat. He slept a good deal. His dreams were regular and kind. Not only did he have a good punch, he could take a punch, too. His reflexes were sound. The stamina was fine. He was blessed with great energy. Other than this cut over his eye and through his eyebrow, he had never been seriously hurt. Despite this big cut in his eyebrow, he was not a bleeder, at least not yet. His skin was *resilient*, like a raincoat, Mike White said. Like an expensive English raincoat. He had resilient skin. He did not bleed easily. He did not tire. He rarely lost his focus. He never lost hope. He never would want to kill himself. He was salt of the earth, Billy Farts said, a blue-collar fighter, a working-class boxer. He was a lightweight, Mike White said. Fast on his feet. Quick with his hands. Sharp with his moves. Speedy with his mind. Alert. Responsive. Clear-eyed. Focused. He was Kid Coole, the next lightweight champion of the world. He was Kid Coole from Sticks, New York, formerly of New York City, Brooklyn and Long Island.

Formerly a delinquent. But now a fighter. A boxer. Part of Billy Faherty's stable. One of the main fighters for the clubs in Sticks and Leathe. An upstate fighter. But soon-to-be a downstate fighter, at the Garden, and maybe Atlantic City, Foxwoods, maybe even Las Vegas. He was a simple, clean, elegant fighter. He was a decent guy. He was not a hard-ass, not criminally minded. He wasn't a nutter, Billy Farts said, sounding very Irish when he said that Kid Coole was not a nutter. He was, Kid was, like Billy Farts said, tough enough. He was also good enough to get himself killed, according to Billy Faherty, Kid was good enough to be killed.

THE MIDDLE ROUNDS

"They all want to become champion. But reality sets in and then you start to become an opponent. And then after you become an opponent, you become a sparring partner."

—Gerry Cooney

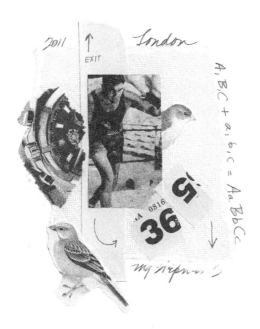

ROUND FIVE

1.

When he woke in the morning, Pearly was gone. There was a knocking in his head. It was the door. A knocking at the door. His head hurt, like a hangover. The day-after a fight. Headaches. Always headaches. Migraines and pains in the muscles. Aches. Like an old man's aches. Like an old woman's. Like having flu. The day after. The day after the fight.

He got up and answered the door.

—Come on come on, Billy Faherty said. Get the lead out of your ass. We got to drive all the fuckn way back to Sticks, Kid.

—Give me a minute, Kid told him, and packed up his gear. That girl...

—What girl?—

Kid put everything in his duffel bag and said he was ready.

—Let's go, Billy Farts said.

2.

They both woke in the middle of the morning. Got up, drank some water. Afterward, they talked:

—You know what my greatest figure is?—

Her tits, her ass, her...

—I don't know.—

—I'm in Mensa, she said.

Kid thought of blood flowing from her. But there was no blood flow.

—It's an organization for geniuses, Pearly said.

—You're a genius? he asked.

—I have a 180 IQ, she said.

—Is that good?—

Pearl smiled.

—I never met a genius, Kid said.

—Now you can say that you fucked a genius in Atlantic City, Pearly told him. I graduated with a three-point-seven-nine grade-point average in Communications Disorders from Rutgers.—

All of this was beyond Kid.

He said:

—Wow!—

—Dean's List, she said. Summa cum laude.—

Then they fell back to sleep.

3.

—Your arms are long, she said.

—I have a sixteen-inch neck and a thirty-five inch sleeve. Everything else on me is compact.—

—You're well hung, she said.

He laughed.

—I'm a Coole, he told her. We're all well hung.

—You got brothers?—

—Have I got brothers!—

—How many?—

—Too many.—

—Which one are you?

—Near the bottom of the litter.—

—Litter?—

—The pile. The heap.—

4.

Kid stood and struck a fighting pose, arms raised, knees bent, center of gravity low to the ground. He had welts and bruises on his face, on his head, his neck, his arms, his chest, his stomach. Big blotchy black and blue spots, making him look like a leopard. One eye was nearly shut, and the other was bloodshot. His nose had a lump on it, so did one cheek.

He grinned like an idiot in a cartoon. If Billy Farts or Mike White were there, they would correct him. It was not his stance but his position. His position was *untenable*, Billy would say. Kid was out of his element. He was winging it. He didn't understand how to behave in such a position. He was with a beautiful naked woman, and yet he did not know how properly to woo her.

—Me, she said, ignoring him. I worry too much.

—I have a thirty-two inch waist, thirty-inch legs on my

pants. My legs and my butt are deceptively thick, though my arms, while wiry, appear thin—

As he said this, he stood in front of the full-length mirror and re-assumed his boxing stance. That was tenable. His stance was right there. He realized that he had never talked so much in his life. It exhausted him in a way that physical activity did not. It crossed his mind that he was not following Billy and Mike's *injunctives*. They had told him not to talk about himself but to inquire about the other person, to ask how she was and to tell him something about who she was. Now Kid had lost the plot. He hadn't asked her anything about herself.

—You're tall, he said.

—I'm almost five feet nine inches tall, she said, looking at herself in the full-length mirror on the closet's sliding doors. I'm, let's see, thirty-five, twenty-six, thirty-five. But I'm a showgirl. What else would I be? I'm, let's see, I wear a thirty-two inch long pant leg.—

As she said these things, she stood in front of the long mirror in the door of the closet that was opened, and she assumed glamorous poses.

—You're all legs.—

—No, look at my breasts. Touch them. Easy. Not so rough. Gently. Gently. That's good. Now kiss them. Good. Not so fast, Kid. Easy, easy. Yes. That's right. Easy. Put your hands on my butt. No, don't stop with your tongue on my nipple. Yes. That's good.—

—Are you gonna come again?—

—I didn't come yet. Only you came, like a little boy, so fast and furiously.—

—I'll come again.—

—Yes, you will come again, my friend. And so will I. So will I.—

Pearly turned Kid over on his back and she hopped on, placing his penis inside of her, and she rode him back and forth, back and forth, with him holding her butt and sucking her nipples, and she let out a big long scream, and then they fell asleep in each other's arms, the air conditioning humming, the porn channel playing, the stereo playing one boy band after another. It was early morning but it was like night. Atlantic City had no morning and night, though, so it was all right.

5.

He would remember her name after they made love and lay in the bed afterward. She had long legs and beautiful breasts and he liked the way they—Kid and Pearl—fit together. She was easygoing, sweet and soft to touch. She was a Latina, a woman from the Bronx and Pee-Aye. He liked her sweet voice, a kind of purr. He liked the way she smelled of herbs and spices. He liked her taste. Lemony. Her breath. Sweet, like her. Her soft neck. Her soft arms, though under them he felt her lean, firm muscles. Pearl had muscles like some of those up and coming women boxers. Some of the women boxers had more muscles than the men. They were harder, though not as strong as the men, and some of them had stamina, but they were not vicious.

None of them had that instinct Billy Farts wanted in all his fighters. What did Billy say? Yes, he wanted gentlemen with a killer instinct. That was Kid all right. He was a gentle man with this instinct to maim others in the ring. In a room such as this hotel room, with this woman Pearl, he lost all those instincts. She was memorable, Pearl was, and she had a significant name, full of jasmine and mango, lavender and oleander, a name of softness and light. She was hard, but he could tell she had no killer in her, no vicious streak, no finishing touch to put away someone. Kid would not forget her. He would not forget her name.

6.

At the end of the evening, tipsy, she followed Kid to his room. He turned on the television to a porn channel, and put on the stereo. She did a striptease for him, only without feathers.

Her breasts were like inflated balloons, perfectly round and big. He'd never seen a woman's body quite like Pearly's, full of curves and incredible muscles.

As Pearly peeled off her clothes, she danced. When she was naked, he noticed that her body was exactly like all the dancers in her routine on the stage. Her breasts were big and hard and round and her ass was big and round and hard and her waist was tiny and she had rippling muscles everywhere, from head to toe. Her figure was like a woman he'd seen in a comic book. Her figure was like Wonder

Woman or something like that. All she needed was a red cape and blue leotards. She was taller than he was, and he rested his head on her bosom as they slow-danced to the porn movie and the stereo music, one of them boy-bands. He could not remember their name. Bands, other fighters, girlfriends. Names were hard to remember. He remembered things like jab. Jab. Jab. Hook. Straight right. Uppercut. He remembered the sound of a particular bird in a particular tree in the backyard of the place where he lived in Sticks, New York. He remembered the smell of the river when he ran alongside of it. He would remember Pearly's smell, too. It had an herbal and a flowery scent, like rosemary, lavender, jasmine, and rose water. He never would forget how her breasts felt, and her nipples. He would remember a little hair in her ear. A mole on her neck. Freckles on her legs. He would remember her all right.

7.

Afterward, Pearly returned. She sat next to Kid, giving him another kiss. She told him that she had seen his fight earlier, and how good he was. He was good, too, and as if she had read his mind earlier, she said that Kid was a kind of artist the way he moved around the ring. She said he was like a choreographer, and he asked her what a choreographer was, and she laughed, saying a choreographer was someone who created all the figures of movement that the dancers executed. Figures of movement that get executed. Now that was what he did in the ring. He severed the ring, breaking it apart, dissecting it in his mind, giving each position of the ring a letter of the alphabet, and in each space he did a different kind of violence to his opponent. He was a choreographer, too, Kid Coole was.

8.

—Are you Cubano? she asked.

—I'm a fuckn American like you, he said.

That made her whoop with laughter.

—He's a fuckn American like me, she said. I love this guy.

Pearly kissed him again, and Kid felt like he was going to burst.

—Where you from? he asked her.

9.

On the drive down to Atlantic City, Billy Faherty and Mike White had told him that if he met any women, he should learn to make conversation with them. Ask them where they were born, where they were from, what they did for a living? Ask them how they were? Pay attention to them. Okay, okay, Kid thought, I can do that. Pearl was a dancer, so he didn't have to ask her that question. He already knew what she did. But he didn't know where she was from or where she was born, but he knew how she felt because she had told him. She felt good, she said. Life was beautiful. So where was she from?

—The Bronx, she said. Me and Jennifer Lopez.

—You know her?—

—Nah, I'm just sayin'. We're both from the Bronx, only I moved away when I was a kid, and my family moved to Philly.—

—Philly's a good town for fighters, Kid said. The Blue Lagoon, he said.

—Blue, no, it's not called Lagoon.—

—Joe Frazier. Philly fighters are tough. They're good.—

—After the Bronx and Philly, my father bought a farm in central Pee-Ay.—

—Pee-Ay, where that?—

She laughed and kissed him again.

—I love you, man. Pee-Ay, it's Pennsylvania.—

—Is that what Pee-Ay means: Pennsylvania?—

—Yeah, man.—

—Shit, Kid said. Live and learn.

She said:

—I love the way you fought. You remind me of the old-time fighters. I watch the classical matches on cable. With my uncles and brothers. I see all the fights in the casinos too. My father worked in boxing. He's dead now. But he worked as a cut-man. Maybe you heard of him. Manuel Ortega Winters.—

—Hey, Mike White, you ever hear of Manuel Ortega Winters?—

Billy said,

—I knew him in New York. Manny Ortega. We was friends, oh, years ago. He died of a bad liver.—

—This is his daughter, Pearly.—

—Your father was a good man, Billy said.

—Thank you, thank you very much.—

Kid saw tears rising in the corner of her eyes. He patted her back. There. There. She put her head onto his shoulder. He smiled goofily at his cornermen who were lost on other matters entirely. They were talking about Carmen Basilio and Gene Fullmer when Pearly began to kiss Kid Coole with her tongue deep in his mouth. The cornermen didn't even notice when she put her hand in his crotch or what he grabbed of her in return.

10.

Pearl came down on a big crescent moon, legs kicking, naked on top, and became the central dancer, with all the other girls fawning over her. Her eyes were big and round, and her headdress was less feathery than the others, though she became naked faster than they did, in fact, became completely naked, and then ascended into the ceiling on the crescent moon, her back arched backwards, her breasts pointing skyward, and she looked right at Kid Coole as she ascended to heaven, blowing him kisses.

After Pearl disappeared into the heavens, Kid lost interest in the show, even though the other showgirls were still strutting their stuff. They were topless and in skimpy panties and red highheels. They wore the big feathery headdresses. It was like a work of art, he figured. They were works of art. Poetry in motion. Things of beauty. There was something mysterious to it. You could not summarize what it was you saw. He could tell all the dancers were well trained. They seemed athletic. Smart. How could a dumb broad remember all those moves? They must be rich. He thought they got paid well. At least they looked like they were enjoying what they did. They smiled in a pleasant way. Their teeth were white and spotless. He liked how smooth and long their muscles were.

The only time he really listened to music was in order to fight. That's what Kid realized listening to the music now. He was not about to fight and he was listening to it, enjoying its pulse and rhythms. He rarely listened to it to soothe his feelings, make him feel good about himself. He never listened to music to dance or enjoy the beat. He listened to rev up, to get excited about doing violence to another person. The showgirls were different. He felt soft and gentle, kind and warm-hearted around them. He felt gigantic and good, a decent human being. Shit, he thought. What the fuck is happening? Did they spike the drinks? He was only drinking a club soda. But maybe they put goofer dust in his drink.

He stared at the naked women dancing only a few feet in front of him.

What they did was to dance around, never bumping into one another. They performed very elaborate dance steps. It was almost like seeing an ice capade show. Only they took off their clothes in Atlantic City. Here and there. Removed some clothes or took off one feather or another feather. The next you knew, they were naked. Without feathers. Still dancing. Still artistic as hell. Brilliant. They were like ballerinas. They did not look like hookers. Kid imagined someone like Pablo Picasso, the painter, drawing them in his studio in Paris, France or wherever his studio was. He imagined Michelangelo, the Italian artist, drawing them in his studio in Florence, Italy. They looked like college-educated, middle-class, wholesomely naked women. And Kid liked it. He liked it very much. It was good. It was very good this dancing around naked like they were models for a famous, great artist. Art must be like this, he thought, a roomful of naked showgirls on display in a dark night-room in Atlantic City.

Art must be as much fun as beating up people.

11.

Frankie Cee introduced Kid to Pearl. He called her Pearly. She had been in the floor-show that they had been watching. It was a great show, Kid thought. A bunch of the women—all of them taller than he was—danced around to a latin beat. The lights were timed perfectly to their swirling movements, the bounce and roll of their hips. Their costumes were great. Skimpy but very tasteful. And they came off so effortlessly. He wished he had a robe that could come off as easily as the dancers took off their clothes.

The band was doing a good imitation of Carlos Santana.

This was not the main stage. It was one of the smaller lounges. The performers were close to all of them. The room was littered with fight people and big-shots from New Jersey, government guys and commission guys, people in the construction trades, cops and firemen, bartenders and waiters off-duty. They seemed to be wearing lots of gold jewelry and silk shirts opened to their navels. Some of them wore white loafers and pale yellow slacks (more than ten of them, he counted), and even a Panama hat here and there. Kid had shown up in a new nylon workout suit, dark blue with a white stripe on the sleeves and down the side of the trouser legs.

—Wait until the next act, Pearly told Kid. I get a showcase scene. You'll see. And I'll come to visit you again after the show.

She kissed Kid on the cheek.

—Oh, Mr. Bigshot, Billy Farts said.

—Pearl's a lovely girl, Frankie Cee said, watching her go off to change.

—She liked you, Mike White observed.

—Go on, Billy Farts said. He said it the Irish way, as if he was saying, You're full of it now.

The showgirls wore ballroom gowns and danced around. As the music became faster, they shed their clothes. Kid was not sure where the feathers came from, but there were lots of them in their headdresses. Feathers covered their body parts. Then feathers drifted away, blowing off them.

They became featherless. Naked as the day they were born. Dancing on the stage even minus the G-strings. They were tall and naked and had perfectly shaped breasts, with big round buttocks. Their legs were long and sleek, and they moved with machine-like precision, dancing and stripping and now naked, humping and bumping, smiling, always smiling. Were they having half as good a time as I am? he asked himself. Nah, he thought. They're working, and you already finished your work.

12.

After the fight, the manager of the casino invited Billy Faherty and Mike White and Ralph Half-Dog and Kid Coole to the floor show.

—On the arm, the manager told them.

His name was Frankie Cee. Kid had seen Frankie Cee. He was often in Atlantic City, New York City, and up in the mountains, either in Sticks or Leathe, checking out the new generation of fighters. Frankie Cee scouted fighters for AC. He probably worked for other people, too. But no one ever mentioned anything about his other line of business.

—Guys with bent noses, Billy Faherty said, winking, once upon a time when Frankie Cee had visited one of their gyms upstate.

Now Frankie walked ahead of them down a long hotel corridor. He stopped and waited for Kid.

—You faced quite an opponent tonight against Rickey "Quickie" Santiago.

Kid could not remember who he fought. Names went in one hole in his head and out the other.

—I'm not good with names, Kid said.

—But Kid's good wiff his hands, Mike White shot back.

—I forget most of the people I fight after it's all over.—

—My kind of guy, Frankie said, hugging Kid. Hey, Billy Farty, remember those boxing commission hearings in New York State where Floyd couldn't remember who he beat to become heavyweight champeen?

—Careful, careful, Billy said. Floyd was Kid's mentor when he was young.

—With all due respect, Billy, with all due respect, Frankie Cee said, raising his hands like a bandit caught at the O.K. Corral or a bank clerk caught taking money from the till. Hey, Billy, you hear the one about the guy who got Irish Alzheimer's? He forgot everything but the resentments. It sounds like you, Billy Farts. You're gonna forget everything but the resentments, my friend.

—I don't have any resentments, Billy said. So don't make me start having them all the sudden.

—I love you guys, Frankie Cee shouted. I love you guys. You're my kind of people.

They all walked single-file down a tunnel through the bowels of the hotel in Atlantic City, working their way to a nightclub in the hotel. The three men talked about Floyd again, and Kid could understand how Mr. Patterson did that. How he might forget the details of his fights, even a championship. Kid rarely remembered any of the other guys he fought. Sure, he would recognize them if he ran into them in a gym, on the street, or down in Jersey at the fights. What he did remember, when he ran into these people, was some quality about them. One might be the Italian, the other the Puerto Rican from the Bronx or the Cuban from Miami. There was the black guy from Syracuse, the black guy from Schenectady, the black guy from Troy, or the one from across the river. Some of them he only remembered as Mr. Low-Blow. Mr. Hip-Puncher. The Guy who stepped on his toes and broke the toe next to the big one on my left foot. Crazy-Eyes. The Guy who spit on him. The Biter, and there were biters long before Iron Mike. The Jewish Guy. The Guy with the Big Feet. The Guy with No-Teeth. Tony Baloney. Mr. Kidney Puncher. Mr. Headhunter. The only fighter's name who Kid could remember was Blue Rivers, and that's because Blue Rivers beat him. That was Kid Coole's only loss. Well, he thought he had won. But later Billy said that Kid hadn't done enough to win the fight. Kid would take care of that matter one day soon. Then he could forget Blue Rivers' name, too. He would never have to recall that name again. Blue Rivers.

13.

Kid showered in the locker room, feeling good, a little sore, but nothing to worry about. True, he pissed blood. But didn't he always piss blood after a fight? Didn't everyone piss blood after they fought? It was no big thing. Sore ribs. Sore hand. Sore cheekbone. Sore head. But not a sore loser, a winner tonight, his first big fight in AC. He had a bruise under one eye, a cut lip, lump on his nose, a sore hand from clubbing the guy all night. It was one of those fights where Kid never really got hurt. The scar tissue over his eye never opened.

14.

The early rounds are even. Then in the sixth round, the guy gets cute, tries to do some fancy footwork, and he starts jawing at Kid Coole, and Kid just hunkers down, and comes underneath him, leveling the guy with an uppercut right on the bottom of the jawline.

The bell saves the opponent—the other guy—and he stumbles to his corner where they try to revive him.

Kid looks over there, trying to see what's going on.

—You forget about his corner, Billy says. This is your corner, sonny. No cute stuff, all right? You see what happens when a guy gets cute, he gets an uppercut on the jaw, that's what he gets for being cute. You listen here, Kid Coole. You got to knock this guy out. The longer you let him stay around, the more dangerous he's gonna become. You're gonna give him confidence that he can beat youse. Who knows what might happen? I don't want to see the fight go that way. His legs are wobbly. When the bell rings, you go out to the center of the ring. Touch gloves. Be kosher. But go to town on him straight away. Knock this fuckhead right out, Kiddo. You understand. Knock this fuckbag of shit out.

Bell rings to start the new round. Kid trots to center of ring. He touches gloves in the center of the ring at the start of Round Seven.

Referee tells them to fight.

There is no juice in the guy, no steam, so Kid sticks him with a jab. Then another jab. He whacks him good with a left hook on the jawbone again. He hits him on the other side of the jaw with a right cross. He goes downstairs. He whacks the guy's sides with two snappy punches, a left to the liver, a right to the spleen. Then he goes upstairs again. He hits him with the jab. He jabs again. Then he unloads an in-close, nasty straight right, again on the jawbone, and the guy falls backwards on the seat of his pants, and the back of his head snaps on the lowest rung of the ring ropes, and the ref has to pull his head off the ropes and count him out cold.

Kid trots back to his corner. There is no war dance, no waving to the crowd.

—Good fight, Mike White says.

—Real good, Ralph Half-Dog tells him.

—You were all right, Billy says. But this is not the champeen of the world. This is a guy like yourself, someone trying to get a ranking. So let's keep it in perspective.

Kid puts the hood of his robe over his head, and stalks out of the ring between Billy in front and Mike and Ralph taking up the rear. No grandstanding. No shenanigans. Billy had instructed him how to leave the ring when they were back in Sticks.

—Be a gentleman, he said. Keep your dignity. You ain't

a big shot yet. You're a fighter from nowhere looking for a ranking. That's all you are right now.

15.

Billy Faherty affected a fight in Atlantic City.

—Pack your bags, he said, we're going to AC.

—Who'm I fighting? Kid asked.

—Don't worry who you're fighting, Billy said, but it will be competitive, more action than you get in Troy. A better opponent than you've faced in Schenectady. You'll be fighting someone who wants to be ranked too. He's going to give you a good fight, and you need to be on your toes. You need a good fight under your belt. But you can win this fight. I don't make matches that I think you're gonna lose.

—You all'll kick some ass, Kid, Mike White said.

—It's no walk in the woods, Billy said. It's fuckn Atlantic City, man.

—Kid's ready.—

ROUND SIX

1.

They left the arena and went into the locker room where Kid showered and changed into a new white nylon outfit of pants and zip-up jacket and a new pair of white trainers. He tucked a short white terrycloth towel around his neck and put on a white baseball cap with the New York Yankees insignia. Over his sore nose he placed a very light pair of sporty wrap-around sunglasses. He packed his gear into a big duffel bag and he met his corner outside the locker room, and together they all walked the couple of blocks to the garage where Mike parked the van. Then they drove home.

The drive back to Sticks went smoothly. When you win, the ride back is quick.

—Am I good? Kid asked Billy.

—You're good enough, he said. You could be better. You could listen to me more. You could be less predictable. But you are good enough, Kid.

—Am I tough? he asked.

—You're tough enough, Billy said.

—Oh, he's tough, Mike White observed.

—He's tough enough, Ralph Half-Dog added.

Ralph was Kid's seat-mate. Mike White drove. Billy sat in the killer seat up front. Ralph and Kid always got the back-seat of the van.

Kid fell asleep in the back of the van. Usually Billy was alert enough not to let this happen. You never want to fall asleep until everything looks okay neurologically. Mike or Billy will ask him who he is, where he was born, who his parents are, where he grew up. What year is it? Who is the President of the United States? Count backwards from 100. But Billy was tired, and he was not paying attention, so the Kid fell asleep. He dreamt about moving backward. When he woke up, they were almost back in Sticks. Billy said, as though finishing a thought that Kid Coole did not hear.

—As long as it is to your advantage.—

—Right, Mike White said.

As they drove up the hill past the prison, Billy turned toward the Kid and said:

—You didn't fuckn fall asleep, you fuckn asshole?—

—Nah, I was dozing, Kid answered him groggily.

—Who are you? Billy asked.

—What?—

—You heard me, he said. Who are you?—

—I'm Kid Coole.—

—Real name.—

—Parnell.—

—Where were you born?—

—Saint Mary's Hospital in Bedford-Stuyvesant, Brooklyn.—

—Count backwards, Billy said, starting at one hundred. Count.

—One-hundred, Kid said, 99, 98, 97, 96, 95...—

—There you go, Ralph said, laughing. I don't think I could do it myself, Kiddo.

They turned down Third Street and into Sticks, and home.

And then they pulled up in front of Kid's boarding house on Poe Street and let him out, giving him his gear and telling him to rest and take a few days off, get back into the gym when he was ready. As the van pulled away and the Kid walked down the gravel driveway toward the back of the big old house where he lived, he saw sets of eyes in the backyard, the deer coming to forage. When they heard his footsteps, they scattered.

He fumbled for his keys on the back landing, still counting. Eight-five, 84, 83, 82...

Up the stairs, around the corner, down the long dark hallway, and fumbling again for his keys, he entered his room, put his gear down, and lay on the bed in his white nylon outfit and his new white trainers and his white Yankee baseball cap. He kept counting, 51, 50, 49...

Then as he drifted off, the numbers reversed themselves, starting at one and going toward ten. One, 2, 3, 4, 5, 6, 7, 8... At eight, he woke in a cold, clammy sweat on the bed, his nylon suit soaking wet, his head aching. His body ached. He groped in the dark for his mouthpiece, but Kid couldn't find it, and he didn't hear the referee counting anymore. Then he remembered that he was home, not in the ring.

2.

Kerry broke away from her mother and ran into the back of the house where her room was. She slammed the door hard, and the house shook from it. Kid could hear her, from the living room, in the back of the house crying.

Kid got up and went into the kitchen and made some dough, letting it rise overnight. In the morning, he would make bread. Eating bread, that was good. Running in the mountains was good. Being alive was good. Being in love was, too. Being a teenager was no good, though. It sucked. That was a kind of pain he didn't want again. He would rather hurt from punches. Hurt from broken dreams and love. He did not want that pain of being a teenager ever again. That was the most painful pain of all. It was worse than jealousy. Worse than black eyes and broken noses. Broken hands and cracked ribs. A fractured jawbone. Fractured arm. Broken skull. Fractured spine.

As the bread rose, he sat on the couch. The cries had diminished to simpers. Gladiola was in another room crying herself. He watched the sports channel. A lightweight contest. He did not like either fighter. But he felt this feeling inside of himself. A boiling point in his gut. He was better than those two. Why were they on television, making money, being written about the next day, and he was here in Sticks, waiting to be ranked when he knew he could take out either one of them in a few rounds?

He wanted to sleep. So he closed his eyes on the couch, and listened to the pulsing in his ears. Blue Rivers. Why?

Why? Why? The pulse asked. Then it was only that name: Blue Rivers. Why? Why? His heart beat. Why? Jab. Blue. Jab. Straight right. Jab. Rivers. Jab. Uppercut. Jab. Hook. Hook. Jab. Cross. Why? Blue. Why did he win the match and why did Parnell Coole end up with one loss on his record?

—You gonna sleep on the couch? Gladiola asked.

—Yeah, he said.

And she turned off the television. Then she turned off the light and went to bed alone. He heard the sobbing from the back room, and then he fell asleep himself.

3.

Kerry came home.

—Hey, how was your night? her mother asked.

—Oh, fuck off, Kerry said.

—Don't talk to me like that.—

—You fuckn losers. Why don't you both get out of my life?—

—I'm your mother.—

—Big shit.—

—What?—

—You heard me, you fuckn loser.—

Whack. Then whack. Whack.

—What?—

—Why don't you kill me, you fuckn psycho!—

—I'm your mother.—

—Big fuckn shit!—

—You need to show some respect.—

—Respect yourself.—

4.

They sat on the couch together, silently watching the movie on the television until a pizza delivery arrived. They ate the pizza without talking. It was a big cheese and tomato pizza. Pizza was his only indulgence as a fighter. Even then, he only ate it once every couple of months. He ate half and she ate half. Then the movie ended. Kid thought she would invite him into the bedroom. But then:

—Choose, she said.

—What?—

—Me or her, said Gladiola.

—You high or what?—

—Choose, man.—

He laughed.

Gladiola punched him hard on the arm. His bicep ached. But he laughed again. Kid loved pain. Pain was his friend. Billy told him that. He said

—Pain's the touchstone of spirituality.—

Kid wanted to laugh. He wanted to tell her that Pearl was gone. She liked the ocean. She was an Atlantic City showgirl.

—Well? Gladiola asked.

Kid had used more words in the evening than he usually did. Words were not his medium. Legwork. Fists. Bob and weave. Pound, pound, pound. Drift away. Set. Jab. Jab. Straight right. That's what Kid knew how to do. He knew how to jab and move. Set and deliver a straight right. His straight right was very good. So was his uppercut. His left hook. His slashing right cross. But words?

—I love you, he said.

—You damn fool.—

—I do, he said.

—You fuckn idiot, she said. I ain't axing you to say anything like that to me.

Her glassy eyes had water pooling at their edges.

—You a damn fool, that's what you are, man.—

Now he figured he'd said too much.

Gladiola kissed him. They embraced on the couch. She cried. He never saw her cry so hard. She kissed him again. More intensely. Then she fiddled with his zipper and pulled down his pants. Took off her own. Hopped on him on the couch. They did it. They made love. Fucked. Fast. Furiously. Wham-bam. Thank you. Then she cried again, and he embraced her. She cried hard. So he cried too. Crying was easy for him. Life was short and painful. Why not cry? He used to cry himself to sleep in the holding cells they put him in before Mr. Patterson took him from Long Island up here to Sticks. He cried in his bed until sleep descended upon him. So crying with Gladiola was easy.

Then like that, they stopped, got up and went about their business in the house. She cleaned up in the kitchen. He watched the news, waiting for the sports to come on.

5.

—What it is? Mr. Kim asked. It is plastic.

The customer held it up, looked at it in the light.

—It looks like glass.—

—Stronger.—

The customer stood in the office part of the factory that was located right on the river in Sticks.

Parnell Coole worked in the warehouse, moving pallets, sweeping, getting orders for customers. His bosses were Koreans, an old man who dressed like a cowboy and his younger wife who wore men's work clothes. The wife used to be a stripper, and the rumor was that Mr. Kim was a retired intelligence officer.

The Kims ran a plastics factory on the edge of Sticks. Kid hauled palettes, took out garbage, ran errands from one end of the factory to the other.

Mr. Kim called the Kid,

—The Shlepper—

Before the plastics factory, the Kims owned a hat-importing warehouse in Brooklyn, where Mr. Kim learned to spice his conversation with Yiddish words, particularly as the Hasidim from nearby Borough Park were his middlemen. The hat factory was in Sunset Park, down by the piers.

Over many lunch breaks in Sticks at the plastics factory, Mr. Kim or his wife Sunny had told the Kid about their hat business in Brooklyn. Mexicans in one part of the warehouse removed a label which read, "Made in China."

Salvadorans in another part of the Brooklyn building sewed a label into the hat's sweat band which said, "Authentic Panama Hat." Cambodians boxed the hats in a third part of the warehouse.

The Kid listened to either Mr. Kim or Sunny tell him about the hat warehouse in Brooklyn. He sensed that they liked hats better than plastics, and Brooklyn more than Sticks.

The Kims often invited Parnell Coole to eat lunch with them. Mr. Kim liked Kid ever since the young fighter told them that his grandfather, Thomas Mojo Moody, had been a haberdasher in Brooklyn before the Depression.

Sunny, the wife, also liked Kid because he reminded her of her two brothers who also had been boxers.

The Kid liked the food mostly, but he especially liked the barley and green tea that Mrs. Kim served them.

Near the holidays Sunny served barbecued beef or short ribs. Sometimes she and her husband ate fish heads. But Kid never joined them. He preferred a nice, clean filet. Once in a while Mrs. Kim served them mackerel. But Kid would decline it.

—In training, he said, patting his stomach. Need to get in shape for a fight.

They ate rice, fermented cabbage (kim-chee), strips of paper-thin seaweed, and beancurd. The food tasted good. He liked it. Afterward it gave him a lot of energy, though the beancurd always made him fart. Pizza made him fart, too. He tried to stay away from pizza before a fight. He knew the real reason why Roberto Duran said,

115

—No mas!—

to Sugar Ray Leonard.

Duran had eaten too much Spanish food just before the fight and he needed to take a shit. All of Leonard's jabs to Duran's stomach made the latin fighter feel as if he might crap his boxing shorts in front of those millions of people watching. So he said,

—No mas!—

Pizza and beancurd were good things to avoid before a fight.

6.

—We aren't even dating, Kid told Gladiola.

—Who? she asked.

—Who?—

—Who are you not dating, Kid, me or her?—

Bubbles of anger. His friend. His girlfriend. He did not know it. Is she it? Muscles of anger. Anger's rippling manner. The anger of the world. Concentrated into her. His friend. His girlfriend. He did not know it. No one told him, not even her, Miss Gladiola. She had seen the fighter walking around Sticks with Pearly from Atlantic City. Nobody in Sticks dressed like Pearly, not even the hookers. She looked like she had been poured into her jeans, and she wore a halter that showed her muscular midriff, even in the cold weather. She wore white cowgirl boots, and a big bright-colored scarf wrapped many times around her neck.

She wore a oystery gray fur coat, and had on wrap-around sports sunglasses.

—Me or her?—

—Both, he said.

—Bofe?—

—Yeah, he answered her, thinking his answer pretty slick.

It was true that he met someone, even if Kid didn't know that Pearl had already dumped him for good. Pearl smoked and drank alcohol, but was also a health nut like he was, only she had these contradictions. But it was also true that Pearly was history. Pearly was gone. How did you explain this to the human dynamo known as Gladiola?

—I'm your friend, she told him, and I'm a girl. I'm a woman.

—Yes, you are, he said, but I'm not your boyfriend. You was the one who told me that.

—You're always over our house, baking bread in my kitchen, sleeping on my couch, taking my kid and me shopping at the malls out Route 9.—

—We're friends, Kid said.

Her eyes were glassy with tears, but they also had a bubbling to them, like the surface of a pot of water just before it boils.

—And the bitch from Jersey?—

—Pearl is from Pennsylvania, Kid told Gladiola, and she works in New Jersey.

Philadelphia, Pee-Ay. Pee-Ay: that's Pennsylvania. She lived on a farm outside Harrisburg. But she was born in the Bronx.

—What's the bitch to you?—

—She's my friend, he said.

—You ain't doin' her?—

—We did stuff, he said.

—I'm axing you a question, dufus.—

—Yeah.—

—You doin' her?—

—I don't see her no more.—

—Where she at?—

—She don't like the mountains.—

—Dumb bitch.—

He sat down for the first time. Put his feet up on the coffee table. Put his hands behind his head. Relaxed. Stretched out.

—So I'm your boyfriend?—

—Did I say that?—

—You *suggesterly* it.—

—What?—

Kid could not pronounce the word correctly, and so he did not say it again.

Suggesterly.

—You crazy, man. You one crazy motherfucker if you think I'm your girlfriend, Gladiola said. Shit! I don't even like men.

—Then why you act so jealous on me?—

—Shit, you crazy, Kid. I ain't jealous on you.—

—I'm gonna be ranked soon, he said.

—Shit.—

—Word, he said.

118

—Word, my ass.—

—I'm gonna be ranked, Gladdis.—

—Don't you call me Gladdis, Kid. I'll whop you upside the head so hard, you forget what day of the week you are in, and where you at.—

7.

Pearly smoked another cigarette, took off her pants and had sex with him quickly on the little bed, and left Sticks for good, getting in her blue Toyota rental car, and drove across the Headless Horseman Bridge to Leathe and then picked up the New York Thruway, driving south toward New Jersey, picking up the Garden State, and then eventually heading to the Jersey shore, and going south into Atlantic City and her condo by the ocean. It wasn't like it used to be, even if she didn't know what it had used to be like. For now, it was okay. It was home. It was where she hung her hat. At least it wasn't Sticks. At least it ain't a hick town in upstate New York, she thought.

—Hey, he lives in Sticks, she said out loud as she drove. He's from the Sticks.

You would not want to hang your hat in Sticks.

That gave her an idea: do a strip act to Joe Cocker or Tom Jones singing "You Can Wear Your Hat." Was that the name of the song? "You Can Leave Your Hat On." Something like that. And when she stripped down to nothing, she'd wear a top hat or a bowler hat or maybe even a baseball hat. No, a very sexy straw cowboy hat, beat up and broken in. She'd be naked, only for the straw cowboy hat. You can wear your hat. You can leave your hat on. Yeah.

—Hey, Kid, she shouted, you can kiss my big pearly ass. Yeah. You can kiss my Cubana ass, man. *Tu sabe, maricon. Coño. Tu sabe, coño.* You can kiss my ass. You can wear your baseball hat when you do it, you hick from Sticks. She laughed hard. You clown from town. This is Atlantic City, man. This is where the best dancers dance. The best fighters fight. The best wiseguys come to be entertained. The best hustlers hustle. The best tits. The best asses. Yeah. You can wear your hat. You can wear whatever you want. You fuckn nobody from Sticks. You can wear your fuckn coat, man. You can close the door from the outside, *coño.*

8.

—I prefer the ocean, Pearly said. Atlantic City has it all.

But in the mountains, Kid worked. The mountains, he told her, was where fighters trained. That's the way it had been, and it was the way he liked it. That's the way it was going to be.

Kid ran harder in the mountains. He punched through there. He moved faster.

—I like the ocean, he said. But I live in the mountains.

Pearl laughed.

They had watched the sun rise over the boardwalk and beach and ocean a few months earlier. Now she was in his tiny room in Sticks, looking out its back window at a yard filled with snow and a few stray deer eating vegetation from the garden. Sticks was nothing like Atlantic City; it had no glitz, no rush, no action. It was as quiet and slow as an old man walking down the street with his little dog and balancing himself on a stick.

Pearl had visited Kid in Sticks and the mountains a few times, but confessed to being bored by it all. She told him it was a dull place.

—I guess if you had a lot of money for antiques, you could walk over to Harding Street and spend it. You could buy a nice piece of linen or a sweet-smelling candle. But what else is there to do? Eat a meal in a restaurant. Go for a walk. Jesus, Kid, what kind of life is that?—

She lit a cigarette: the first person to smoke in his little room.

But he did not object.

Pearl looked out the window at the deer in the back yard.

—A depressing place, she said.

It was not his intention to defend Sticks. If she did not like it, that was fine with him. Kid liked it. If it was dull or depressing, he did not care. It was a hideout, a sanctuary, the place where he trained to fight. He could walk the several blocks to the gym to train with Billy and Mike and Ralph. What did she know? She probably only knew a handful of things about boxing. How to position your feet. Balance. How to jab. Set up the big punch with the jab. Set up the jab with the movement. How to throw a straight right. The knockout punch.

9.

—I got to get out of here, man.—

—So go, he said.

—What you say?—

—Go.—

—That any way to talk to me?—

—You don't like it, he told her. Go.

—Hey, fuck you, Jack.—

—I'm just sayn you don't have to stay here. You can go.—

—I'm axing you a question first. Why you like it here?—

—It's where I train.—

—But what you do when you ain't training?—

—Nuffink.—

—Weird.—

—I don't do nuffink but train.—

—You weird.—

—Hey, what can I say, he said.

—You weird, man.—

BETWEEN ROUNDS
(ONE-MINUTE IN THE CORNER)

II.

I knew how to slip and slide, didnt I, didnt I, & I knew the drill about duckn the jabs and slippin the power, and never dreamt it wd be a sucker punch that deadened my senses and made me cock/eyed like Popeye after Bluto ran off with Olive Oyl. They say that the punch you never see is the one that will get you, will floor you, turn you all around, and they are right about that one. I never saw it comin, thought this dance wd go on forever and a day, but this guy danced me into a corner, then he hit me with a kidney punch that put me on Christopher Street, lights goin out.

1.

He sat on the porch of the nursing home next to his auntie. Aunt Ella had gotten old, not before her time, but right on time, though she had become much older than the last visit to the home. Uncle Tony, her brother, the fighter, the prisoner-of-war, he was old prematurely, only he still looked like a dopy teenager. Kid was young and alive. But, he could be one fight, even one punch away from old age. He could be rocking next to Aunt Ella and not even know it was his aunt next to him.

—*I'm being taken care of, she said.*

—*You're all right in my book, the Kid told his aunt, patting her hand.*

—*What book is that?*

—*How the fuck would I know? Kid said, shrugging his shoulders.*

They laughed.

—*How the fuck would you know? she repeated, only putting slightly different emphasis on each word.*

The couch on the porch at Ralph Half-Dog's house sagged. It sat on the outdoor porch of his house, soggy and sagging. His porch also sagged. And so did the street. It sagged, too. Muhammad Ali Way sagged. It dipped. It sagged like the couch on the porch. His building on Muhammad Ali Way sagged, too, just like the street, which dipped in front of Ralph Half-Dog's double-decker, two-family house.

Mike White, Ralph's father-in-law, lived with his wife Sapphire on the second floor.

Ralph Half-Dog owned a small bar at the end of the street and around the block. It was called the Neutral Corner. He said he named it after a famous saloon in the City that stood across the street from Stillman's gym where all the great fighters trained.

—That was Whitey Bimstein's territory, Ralph Half-Dog said.

It was almost like he was talking about Saint Francis of Assisi.

Other cornermen received Ralph's adoration too. They included Jack Blackburn—Joe Louis's trainer. He also liked Eddie Futch. Angelo Dundee. Lou Duva. Manny Steward. Cus D'Amato. Gil Clancy. Kevin Rooney. Teddy Atlas. If Ralph said Whitey Bimstein with the love and devotion one might accord St. Francis, these other names were like some of the twelve apostles of boxing.

2.

When Kid went with Aunt Ella as a young boy to visit her brother in Yonkers, they sat on a porch like this one, and in rocking chairs, only instead of the rolling hillside going down to the river, they looked out on the thruway cutting through Yonkers. Ella's nursing home wasn't exactly idyllic either.

On the other side of the house, there was a cement plant that belched out smoke, and Kid smelled an acrid soot in the air. The cement plants, up and down the river, burned old tires and waste, fouling the air, but—they're exempt from environmental laws—his aunt said, the environmentalist, the rabble-rouser. That's what Aunt Ella told him the last time he visited her. The cement plants were exempt from environmental laws.

Ralph Half-Dog weighed in excess of four-hundred-and-seventy-five pounds. They once weighed him on a truck scale alongside the New York State Thruway. He wore his jet-black hair in a ponytail because he was Mohawk. Dressed up, dressed down, Ralph wore bib overalls. Sometimes he wore a tee-shirt or sweat shirt. Other times, his big chest was bare.

He had been a great middleweight in the amateurs.

When he turned pro, he had twenty or so fights. Then he experienced a detached retina. He caught it at the end of a big right. His opponent doubled up off a jab. One right followed by another.

The second right detached his retina. It fell away from its network of arteries.

Ralph was blind in one eye.

The weight came on a few years later. A thyroid problem. He took medication. Ate well. Even walked every day. Nothing helped.

His wife Penny Half-Dog was Mike and Sapphire White's oldest daughter. She was a product of Sticks. She was big, too.

So was Mike and Sapphire. All of them had diabetes now.

Ralph bought the two-family on Muhammad Ali Way and put Penny's family upstairs after their house burnt to the ground a few blocks over on Catskill Street.

Mike and Sapphire didn't pay rent. Ralph let them do all the cooking for the building. Mike White cooked without sugar and salt, a restricted diet to help all of them with their diabetes.

3.

—*I'm not happy, she said. I'm old and I got pains in places I didn't even know I had.*

Then she decided to change the subject.

—*How's your family?*—

—*Fine.*—

—*Fine, she said. Fucked-up, insecure, neurotic, and emotional.*

They laughed. His aunt must have said this every time he visited her. Fucked up. Insecure. Neurotic. Emotional. Yeah, he was fine all right. He was super-fine.

As a couple of Billy Faherty's fighters sat on the sagging couch on the porch, Mike and Sapphire worked two barbecue pits in the side yard next to the two-family. The side lot belonged to Ralph and he used it as his backyard. Another two-family had been there before it burnt to the ground. Ralph bought the land from the former neighbors, who moved away after finding a house in Troy, further upstate. The barbecue pits were set up near the peeling white picket fence near the street. The pits were made from oil drums that were sliced vertically in half. Mike welded legs on them and put industrial chicken wire over the pit. He added smokestack vents on each pit.

Sapphire cooked Southern. Her station produced ribs, fried and barbecued chicken, along with collard greens, blackeyed peas, hot-pepper cornbread, wild rice, and sweet potato pie. For one day, they would not worry about their restricted diets.

Mike attended to a goat stew on a back part of his grill. On the front part he made steaks and grilled vegetables. He heaped the steak with onions and peppers and steak sauce.

He handed Kid a big sirloin cut and said:

—Remember how I told you to eat it.—

—I chew it, then spit out the meat.—

—Yeah, Mike said, like the Mongoose.—

Mike White said Archie Moore was the greatest light-heavyweight who ever lived. Kid's favorite Mongoose fight was when he fought Yvonne Durrell. His second favorite was when he fought Rocky Marciano for the heavyweight championship. Even though Archie Moore lost that fight, he nearly took out Marciano with one of his punches before the Brockton Bomber came out and took care of business. Kid and the other young fighters watched the matches obsessively on DVDs and old tapes.

—Rocky was the greatest inside fighter ever, Mike said.

4.

They sat on the porch and they rocked in their rockers, him and his auntie. Kid pictured members of his extended family. If he went down to the city to be a sparring partner, he called one of them. But other than sparring, he hadn't fought in the city yet. That's what Billy Faherty was trying to do, what he called, affect *a fight in New York City.*

—*I want to* affect *a fuckn fight, Billy said, in fuckn New York City. I want to fuckn* affect *it. Fuckn A.*

Kid thought that Billy Faherty had a way with words, an affinity for them, Billy called it, as he hadn't had the words punched out of him.

—Touch me.—
—No.—
—Why?—
—You're jailbait.—
—Let me touch you.—
—No.—
—Why?—
—I have to fight.—
—So.—
—So, no sex before a fight.—
—Why?—
—Why?—
—Yeah, why?—
—Energy.—
—Energy?—

—Takes it away.—

—You lose your focus?—

—Yeah.—

—How 'bout a hug?—

—Hug's okay.—

—You're like so skinny and yet you're like a rock.—

—In shape.—

—You got no fat.—

—Fat butt.—

—No, you got nothn.—

—Behind my neck.—

—What?—

—There's a roll of fat there.—

—You got a big neck for such a skinny guy, Kid.—

—Need it.—

—You ever gonna stop fightn?—

—Soon.—

—One, two fights.—

—When I become Champ.—

—Or what else?—

—Billy says a person only has so many fights in them. Once you reach your limit, you might as well leave. Otherwise, you are gonna get your ass handed to you on a platter.—

—That's the most I ever heard you say.—

—That's the most I'm ever gonna say.—

—Well, I'm glad I heard you.—

—I'm glad you did. Hey, what are you doin?—

—Just gettin' friendly. You saved my life.—

—You're jailbait.—

—This ain't sex, silly. This is foreplay. This is warm-up. This don't count.—

—It feels like it counts.—

—Don't it feel good?—

—Yeah.—

—Don't you like it?—

—I don't want to go to jail.—

—You ain't gonna go to jail just because someone sucks on you, man.—

5.

—Talk, talk, talk, Mr. Kim said, eating his lunch. Always talking and talking.

—You shut up, you crazy old Kim!—

—Too much words in her head, Mr. Kim said, pointing to his wife's curly black hair.

A black beauty parlor on Harding Avenue in Sticks had given Mrs. Kim an Afro.

Sunny Kim usually wore a pair of carpenter jeans and a plaid flannel shirt with American flag suspenders and Red Wing boots. It was impossible to imagine her in her stripping days, with a G-string and a feather boa and pasties.

Mr. Kim had the weary look of an old cowboy. He reminded Parnell Coole of Gary Cooper or Clint Eastwood, one of those silent, angular people who spoke only a few words in their entire lifetime. The Kid liked Mr. Kim because, unlike his own brothers and sisters, Parnell did not have much use for words either.

He drank the green tea with barley and enjoyed the earthy after-taste it left in his mouth. His boss drank a glass of beer instead of the green barley tea.

Sometimes Mr. Kim backed it up with a shot of Irish whiskey. He drank any kind of cheap Irish whiskey they sold in the liquor store.

—Big headache in Brooklyn factory, Mrs. Kim said, sighing. It was that Boxing-Man-with-Bushy-Hair.

—Don King? Kid asked.

Kid had been trying to meet Don King for years. But Don King wouldn't give Kid the time of day. Mr. King did not like lightweight fighters, Kid was told. Worse than being white or whatever it was Kid was, he was a lightweight. Lightweights didn't draw big money unless you were Manos de Piedra, Sweet-Pea, or pretty-faced Oscar, the really great names from the division. Mayweather or Rosario.

I'm white, the Kid thought, and I'm light.

He once told Mrs. Kim his theory, but she thought it foolish. The notion that being white was a liability for anything in life made no sense to her. Also, she wasn't quite so sure that Kid Coole was white. He wasn't exactly black. He certainly wasn't Korean. But he didn't seem white either.

—You get hit the head too much—

Was how she put it.

Sunny ate her kim-chee and rice and went on with her story about the factory in Brooklyn.

—Man-with-Bushy-Hair come to Sunset Park factory and tell us to get out of Brooklyn with our Chinese Panama hats. He say he have the market on corner—

—The corner on market, Mr. Kim corrected her.

—Yes, Mrs. Kim agreed.

—Corner on market.—

Then she continued.

—However, she said.

—Don King? the Kid asked again.

—Man-with-Bushy-Hair, she repeated, but never actually said it was Don King.

—You talk talk talk, Mr. Kim said. All the time talk talk talk.

He took his hand and made his fingers into a mouth and animated them into a cartoonish way of talking as if his hand were a puppet.

The man with the bushy hair, whoever he was, came into the old factory in Brooklyn with some of his associates, telling the Kims that he had exclusive rights to all Chinese Panama hats in America.

Mr. Kim had called his own people in for advice. Intimidation was not something to bother him. He seemed to like it. Gangsters might have brass knuckles, knives and guns. Mr. Kim knew people with handgrenades, tanks, and fighter jets. But his own associates told him to let go of the hat business.

That's when the Kims moved to Sticks and opened the plastics factory. The hat business was easy. Making plastics was work. You had to produce a product. You had to be at work six days a week.

6.

—Is your sister Sam still married to the garment district fellow?—

Kid came back to the nursing home, back from that place where he had been, back in the gym, sparring, back in the ring, running up his record, only still trying to rectify, Billy said, that one loss to Blue Rivers. He looked at his aunt, smiled, searched for the word.

—Divorced, he said.

—And she never remarried?—

—Married another garment district guy, and they been together twenty years.—

—That's the one I'm talking about.—

—The second one?—

—Yeah, the second fuckn one.—

—They're doing all right in Florida, he said.

—His family were shylocks for the mob, right?—

Kid shrugged his shoulders as if to say he didn't know. He learned a long time ago it was better not to know such things. And if you did know, it was better not to say anything. People talked too much anyhow. He liked to be silent about such matters. Who knew or cared if his sister's husband's family were shylocks for the mob? Who knew what his brother Emmett really did? Who knew what happened to his twin brother Rory? Or their father: what did their father do down the piers? These were not things that a young fighter needed to know about. He would live to be an old man not knowing any of that shit. He would live well without these worthless details in his head.

Four small boxers, including Kid Coole, sat on the sagging couch on the porch. They ate mashed potatoes, beans, cornbread, and steak.

Each had a plastic cup he or she spat the steak grizzle into.

One of the fighters was a young woman from Leathe named Carmen O'Reilly, an up-and-coming boxer. The other two fighters were Carlos Brown and Sonny Boy Johnson. Both were from Bedford-Stuyvesant, Brooklyn. Sonny Boy had once been a champion.

Ralph was on the other side of the lawn, towards the back of the house and the alley. There was a garage back there. One of his friends had set up a keg of beer. It was put there because Billy Faherty and Mike White were recovering alcoholics and didn't drink anymore. Both attended AA meetings at a church in the middle of Sticks, sometimes going every day. To show his respect, Ralph Half-Dog made everyone who wanted to drink do it in the alley, not on the lawn where everyone was eating.

In the middle of the lawn Billy Faherty and his wife Mary Sullivan talked with Ralph's friends. Nearly everyone at the party was involved in the fight business.

7.

—*Remember my brother? she asked.*
—*Yeah.*—

—He was a fighter.—

—Yeah.—

—You are too, she said, tapping his shoulder with a playful punch.

It's getting time to go, he thought.

—You're a good boy, she said.

Ralph came up on the porch. The stairs creaked under his enormous weight. He motioned for all the small fighters to get up.

—I'm feeling uncomfortable, he said.

He lay on the sagging couch.

—What're ya doin', Ralphie? Penny asked, coming up the steps behind her husband.

Penny wore quilted oven mittens and carried a spatula.

The porch almost gave way under their combined weight. But Kid knew from the various kinds of jobs he took that wood can take a lot more stress than brick or stone or steel.

—I'm uncomfortable, Ralph repeated himself.

Penny was a nurse, and Ralph had a funny pale-green color. He said his left arm tinkled and ached. He had no feeling in his fingers. His head was dizzy.

—I'm nausatatious, he said, and then he sat up and threw up all over the porch.

He had a seizure. He went into convulsions on the floorboards of the porch.

—Call the ambulance, Penny shouted.

Kid ran inside and called the fire department and told them that Ralph Half-Dog was having a heart attack or a stroke.

When he got back outside everyone stood around the sagging couch as Penny administered CPR to Ralph.

Half the people in the yard were certified in CPR. You couldn't work a corner in New York State without knowing it. So it was a good place to be ill. A good place to have a heart attack or stroke.

The ambulance raced down Muhammad Ali Way a few minutes later. But it took six of the biggest people at the party to lift Ralph Half-Dog into the ambulance.

—Don't worry, Mike White said. Let's keep eating. Ralph had some *agita*. Also, Ralph would want his friends to enjoy themselves, no matter what happened.

Penny left with the ambulance, and a few others raced off in their cars to the hospital on the other side of Sticks.

The small, young fighters chewed their steaks, sitting on the sagging couch, and they spat the meat into their plastic cups. They swallowed the juice, just like Archie Moore, the Mongoose. The party went on. But they all had worried looks on their faces. They seemed moody and sullen, anxious and uncertain about Ralph Half-Dog, whom everyone knew and loved. Ralph worked all their corners.

—Ralph gotta lose some weight, Carmen O'Reilly said between chewing and spitting.

Carmen was very pretty for a fighter. But that would not last long. She'd get some lumpy eyebrows and a bent ear, just like the little guys she sat with.

—We all gotta watch our weight, Sonny Boy Johnson said.

Sonny Boy was thinking of becoming a middleweight

because it was harder and harder to make his welterweight limit.

Carlos Brown was a flyweight and never worried about anything.

Kid Coole stayed the weight he was no matter what happened or what he did. Of course, he didn't drink alcohol, smoke cigarettes, or take drugs. He didn't eat junkfood either. No potato chips or pretzels, no bagels or crullers or jelly donuts. Kid also did what Mike White told him to do. He chewed the sirloin and spat out the meat. He swallowed the juice.

8.

They watched the river below. The Indians called it a river that flowed two ways. That's because it was not a river but an estuary, Billy Farts said. Estuaries were sensitive to the ways of the moon, like the oceans were, Billy added. (Mike White told Kid that one evening as they stood on the edge of the Hudson River in Sticks, looking out at the backward flowing current.) If you watched long enough, the river moved north. Then it moved south. Kid knew how to flow forward and back, and sideways. He knew how to back up when it was to his own advantage. Billy Farts taught him that, too. He was no river like that fellow Blue Rivers, his one loss. There was a perpetual motion about Kid, even if by the smallest degrees. This was just such an example. He needed to be going, not staying still; he needed to get up—and go. He needed to affect a change back

to Sticks. He needed to fight Blue Rivers again and rectify that
one loss.

—You're a good boy, Aunt Ella said, squeezing his hands.

He pulled away from her.

He did not like people squeezing his hands.

9.

When Mr. Kim talked to a customer, he became excited. The light caught the reflection of one of the many rings he wore on his fingers. He removed a four-by-six-inch plastic transparency, the laminate, he called it.

—It's bulletproof, Mr. Kim said, handing the transparency to the customer.

Years ago Mr. Kim was the first Korean to go to China since Mao had taken over after World War II.

—After the Berlin Wall fell, Mrs. Kim said.

But Parnell Coole had no interest in facts. They gave him a headache. History was history. As far as he was concerned, there was nothing but right now. He was here. That's all he knew. He was alive and he was breathing. An energy ran through his veins. He had his health. He still could fight in a ring. He had no interest in China or Berlin, their walls or their people, unless he was to fight one of them in the ring. His trainer had told him that the legs were the first thing to go on a fighter, and the Kid still had his legs. He did his roadwork every morning before the sun came up. He ran four or five miles, depending on the route, through the streets of Sticks, long before he went to work. Kid lived for the moment when he entered the ring and pounded on another human being's body, knocking an opponent into submission. Everything else was a distraction.

A ten-wheeler from Queens was due that afternoon, but not for another hour. Kid was in charge of getting the truck loaded with palettes filled with the transparencies. He stood outside the factory on the loading dock, looking out toward the river and the big mountains beyond, dreaming of fights he had and those to come. When those thoughts left his head, there was nothing there to replace them. He stood there blankly looking off toward the mountains and the river, seeing nothing, as if it were one big transparency. He imperceptibly shuffled his feet back and forth, rolling his head side to side, as if to loosen the muscles before a fight.

He waited for the bell to ring.

ROUND EIGHT

1.

Dear God, Parnell prayed, give me a rematch with Blue Rivers. Make such a fight possible. My body is hard and *elemental*, Billy Farts says. I have no distracting thoughts. I am focused on my daily program. I work. I sleep. I eat. I train. I often think of this one loss in my career. How do I *rectify* it, Billy Farts has asked me. How to *rectify* it. Dear God. If there are women to see, I date them. Sometimes I go to bed with them. Often I say good-night and go home with a peck on the cheek. Once in awhile, I have another professional fight. Then I rest afterward. I rest even when it is not Sunday. This is how fighters live, dear God. We rest after we fight, sometimes for a week or two or even a few months if our bodies are really tired and beat up. When the aches and pains leave my body, I return to the gym. I spar with ranked fighters and even champions. I become their sparring partner. I am not a fancy guy. I don't put on any airs. Even though I am looking for a ranking, I will spar with champeens and ranked fighters. Dear God, make me strong and energetic. Make me an instrument of goodness and strength. Relieve me of my fears. Take away any thoughts and ideas that distract me from my purpose of fighting. I am a holy warrior. Make me scary and dangerous to my opponents, but a good sparring partner and stablemate. Let me be of service to Billy and Mike and

Ralphie, I mean Penny, and the others. Take away any evil thoughts I have. I am yours to shape and do with me as you wish. You are God; I am your servant.

2.

The Commission said that Kid needed a rematch with Blue Rivers in order to become part of the box-off for the lightweight championship. Kid was now twenty-two and one. Blue Rivers was eighteen and seven, yet he took Parnell Coole the distance. He took Parnell to the limit—and won.

—Horses for courses, Billy Farts said. Parnell is infinitely better than this shithead from Albany.—

—Schenectady.—

—Excuse me, Schenectady.—

—But you were saying…—

—I was saying that there were horses for courses. There are fighters for arenas. Blue Rivers is a Troy fighter.—

—Schenectady.—

—Sche-fuckn-nectady. Excuse me again, Mikey. If Kid fought Blue Rivers in Syracuse, if he fought him in Binghamton, if he met him in New York City, Las Vegas, or Atlantic City, Kid Coole would murderize this fuck from Troy.—

—Schenectady.—

—Whatever, whatever. Kid would crematize this motherfuckn bum.—

—But we have to fight Blue Rivers in Schenectady, Billy.

Are you saying Kid could lose there?—

—I'm saying that if I had my way, Kid would only fight this guy in any place but Schenectady. When Kid Coole dies, his tombstone's gonna say: I'd rather be in Schenectady. That's the only time he would rather be there. He isn't gonna get knocked out by this fuckn Rivers. But Kid Coole isn't gonna win on pints neither. He can't win on pints.—

—Pernts?—

—Yeah, pints.—

—Shit, Bill.—

—Otherwise, Parnell Coole is going to be out of the boxing fraternity.—

—But Kid Coole be so good.—

—Which goes to show, Billy Farts said, that being talented is only one part of being a champeen. Some of it is luck, keeping in mind that luck favors the prepared. Some of it is your corner, your management, guys like you and me, Mike White, and some of it is...—

—Horses for courses.—

3.

Blue Rivers looked a little bit like Sugar Ray Robinson. His hair was conked. He was tall and thin, wiry and very muscular and strong. He had a big, radiant smile, and he swaggered. Easy in his bones. All street. Cock of the walk. If you could become a champion on looks, Blue Rivers was the man. Blue would be the unified lightweight champion of the world. He was handsome and stylish, and he looked like a fighter from another era, like the 1940s, when there were really great fighters. It was his *demeanor*, Billy Farts said. It was his *demeanor* that beat Kid Coole that first fight. At the end of the six-round fight, Blue Rivers was the only person in the ring who looked like he had just won a boxing match. Kid Coole looked exhausted and confused, unsure of himself, certainly not a champion fighter, not even a ranked one, not even a real fighter yet.Now they would fight ten rounds. Those four extra rounds made it a very different kind of fight than the first one. Looking good would help Blue Rivers through the first six rounds of their rematch. But looks wouldn't help Blue from Rounds Seven to Ten. This is where Billy and Mike had been training Kid Coole. If the second fight might appear like the first one through the first six rounds, Parnell Coole planned to introduce a new fight from the seventh round onwards.

—Speed and combinations, Billy Farts said. Angles. Blue can look good. But you are going to give him a lot of looks. You're gonna double jab for six rounds, then single jab after Round Five. You're gonna double up on everything else. One right follows another right. One left follows another left, and so on and so forth. You're gonna give him angles. You're never gonna be in front of this fucker. You're gonna confuse him.

Blue Rivers had beaten Kid Coole already, so he was not sweating this fight. This was no big deal to him at all. He expected to beat this Parnell Coole easily once again. He would do the same things he did in the first fight. He would jab. Slap him around. Be everywhere but where Kid Coole expected him. He would give this Kid Coole angles. He would smack smack smack, then be out of there. He would tease him with his long reach, holding him off like Kid Coole was a little bratty kid.

Horses for courses, Billy Farts said, and Blue Rivers was a fighter made for Schenectady.

4.

Kid's hands were taped by Billy Faherty in front of an assistant commissioner who signed the tape. But they were not exactly in Madison Square Garden. He was fighting upstate still. It was a makeshift arena in Schenectady, nowhere nearer the City than his other fights, and yet even people from the City had come upstate to see this fight. The bout would be written about in the New York City papers the next day. ESPN was to video-tape it, possibly to run it the following week if time allowed in one of their other fight-nights.

—Don't wash your hands, Mike White joked.

But Parnell Coole did not feel like joking. He was irritable with everyone.

Nothing pleased Kid before a big fight. He didn't even like Gladiola. Didn't like her kid Kerry. He didn't like Mr. Kim from the plastics factory where he worked occasionally. Didn't like Mrs. Kim and her fuckn kimchee. Didn't like Sticks or Leathe or anything in the river valley where he lived. Kid didn't like the food in the hotel restaurants. He didn't like the waiters or waitresses or even the busboys. Didn't like the bed. The elevators. The patterns on the rugs. The paint on the walls.

—I want you to stick and move, Billy Faherty said.

Mike White kneaded Kid's shoulders.

—I'm going to fight him, Kid said.

Billy Farts looked from Kid to Mike White and he shrugged his shoulders as if to say,

—What am I going to do?—

Then Billy got down to business. He put his face close to the Kid's. He stuck his finger out and nearly poked his fighter in the eye as he waved it to make his point.

—It's good to get worked up before a big fight, Billy Faherty said. I like when you concentrate your energies on the match. I appreciate the enthusiasm. You're motivated. Okay. Fighter should be motivated before a fight. I feel motivated too. But I don't have to tell you that I'm your trainer, and if you are gonna win, you listen to what I have to say. *Capish*?

—What're you saying? Kid asked.

—Jab, jab, Billy said, dancing on his toes and jabbing the air. Get on your bicycle. Move around. Jab and move. Stick 'im. Stick him in the face. Wack him in the sides. Hit him hard. Okay. But then move away. Keep moving this fight. I'm tellin' you. You need to keep moving, sonny-boy. You heard of ba-da-bing from *The Sopranos*, Billy said. This is ba-da-boom. You stick. You move. You don't stand around waiting for the *gabagoo*. This ain't a picnic. This is a fuckin' fight.

You get cute tonight, and you can forget about everything. You get cute with Blue Rivers, and you're history. You don't get to that champeen round one or two fights away.

5.

Kid's in the ring a good five minutes before Blue Rivers enters it. Blue hasn't broken a sweat. Kid notices he's wearing white boxing shoes with tassels. Once again, Blue looks stately—regal.

Penny White Half-Dog, the new spit bucket lady, winks at Kid Coole. He winks back at her. She is a big, pretty woman.

She mouths the word *sweat* for him before the bell rings. Billy and Mike don't see her do this. Billy puts the mouthpiece in Kid's mouth. Mike keeps rubbing his shoulders to loosen them up. Kid winks at Penny again. He turns to face Blue Rivers.

The bell rings.

Kid attempts to touch gloves when they reach the midpoint at center of the ring. But Rivers wings a right at Kid's head which Kid slips. But then Kid gets hit with a slashing uppercut and, off balance, he wobbles backwards.

Blue Rivers jabs. Jabs. Moves right. Sets. Jabs again. He hooks a left into Kid's side. Then he follows with a right into the other side of his body. Right away Kid has that feeling like the first fight. This guy Blue is nowhere where Kid's punches are, and everywhere where Kid does not expect him to be. Blue is everywhere and nowhere at once, jabbing, raising welts on Kid's cheeks, his eyebrows. But Parnell Coole cannot adjust to him.

The bell rings to end the round.

Kid looks for his corner.

He walks towards Blue's corner.

He hears Billy Farts screaming at him across the ring.

He turns. He sees Penny Half-Dog waving and smiling to him, and he goes over to say hello to her.

He sits on the stool expecting a compliment from Billy Farts.

Instead, his trainer says

—Now what the fuck were you doing out there?—

6.

Blue Rivers opens a cut over Kid Coole's right eyebrow in the next round, and Mike White works on it frantically between the rounds.

The blood streams out.

Blue Rivers keeps hitting Kid Coole in those two places in Round Three. Blue whacks him there. Eyebrow / cheek. Cheek / eyebrow. Eyebrow. Cheek. Cheek. Eyebrow. Eyebrow. Eyebrow. Cheek.

If Blue moves left, Kid can't see him. Blue moves left. He hits Kid hard on the side of his head.

Kid's not a talker in the ring. But he can't resist asking,

—You call that a punch?—

A big mistake.

The talking distracts Kid Coole.

Blue Rivers lands the best punch of the fight.

It is a hard straight right to the temple. A knockout kind of punch. But Kid is moving away from it when it strikes.

They say it is the punch you don't see which knocks you out. Kid staggers around the ring until the bell rings to end the round.

He turns to look for his corner but can't find it. Where's Ralph Half-Dog? Where is that humongous Indian? Ralph, big and friendly, would motion him to the corner. But he doesn't see Ralphie Baby.

Then Kid sees Penny Half-Dog waving.

—You all get your ass over here, she shouts.

He sits down.

—You get cute, Billy Farts says, you pay for it. Why are you lettin' this bum hang around? Put him away, Kid.

Kid takes water from a sponge. Spits blood. Drinks some more water. Swallows. He stands and waits for the bell. The pounding heart quiets. He's ready. Heartbeat from 180 to 50 in one minute flat. Now it goes back up again.

—Put him away, Kid, Penny White Half-Dog screams.

He looks at her and he winks. She blows him a kiss. Big Penny. His lucky Penny.

—We love ya, she says.

—What the fuck are you sayin'? her father asks.

—Cut the magillah, Billy says, and fight.

The bell rings.

He trots out.

153

Kid moves left. He moves left again. Then right. Left again. People boo. They paid to see a fight, not a modern dance concert. Kid looks like a one-eyed monster. A Cyclops. Blue blasts Kid with a left hook. Then he follows with a straight right.

Kid falls.

Blue spins and walks crisply to a neutral corner.

The ref counts as Parnell Coole staggers to his feet.

He receives an eight count.

The ref looks carefully into his eyes. Is the fighter still there? Can he continue? Ref decides that the fight will continue. He waves Blue out of the neutral corner, and the fighter trots quickly back to center ring to pound away at Kid Coole.

7.

—You're down too many rounds to win this by pints, Billy says.

—Huh?—

—You need a knockout, the cutman Mike White says.

—Yeah?—

—You need a miracle! Billy Farts says.

8.

—Kid, I said.

—I said it to myself. I said Kid. Kid you are in big trouble. I moved to the left. He moved to the right. I move to the right. He moves to the left. He's on me like stink on shit. He's on me like honey on a bee's ass. He's on me night and day. Day in and out. Night after night. He grabs me and pushes me around. Has his way with me. Turns me into his bitch. I'm his sissy little thing. I wake up, he's in my face. I go to sleep at night, he's standing next to my pallet. He jumps on my back. He gets my head and twists it around like I was a rag doll.

—Try to run, he runs after me.

—Try to back-pedal, he turns on the forward gears.

—I slip, he slides. I slide, he slips.

—I throw a right; he counters with the left. His left lands right flush on my jawbone. Feels like he broke something. He got the nerve dead-on. I throw a left to counter him. He counters with a right. He lands the right right on the top of my temple. I got a headache like a Mack truck ran me over. I'm seeing double. My vision blurs. I'm trying to clear my eyes, but he keeps peppering the eyes with his jab and then his left hooks and the occasional right cross to finish the job.

—My eyebrows are swollen. They break open with a blood-burst.

—I know that my eyebrow is going to burst again any moment. The guts of my eyeball are going to fly in his face.

The guts of my eyes and parts of my front brain are going to spray on the canvas. The brain matter flies onto the tuxedos of the men in the front row and down the cleavage of a woman in an evening dress with spangles on it.

—My arms are like two brick walls.

—Legs feel like lead.

—Head feels like dead.

—Heart is not in it at all.

—Wake up, Kid, I say. Wake up and get the lead out of your pants. Get the lard from your ass. Get into gear, Kid. The time is ticking down. What round is it? What day is it? Who am I?

9.

—Quit fuckn around, Billy says. You're wastin' our time. This guy's got you on a chain like a monkey.

—What I gotta do, Bill?—

—For one thing, shut the fuck up when I'm talkn. Shut the fuck up and let me talk. Two, come underneath his jab. His whole left side is open for a big body shot. T'ree, soon as you body-snatch, you're still down there, use the uppercut. Your uppercut's looked good last coupla fights. Use the fuckn thing. Use the fuckn god-given thing, son.—

—I hate this fuckn guy, Bill.—

—You don't hate nobody. You just go out there and fight. Hate's gonna drain what energy you got left. You don't fight this moron angry. He'll eat you alive. What the fuck round

156

is this? Billy says. What happened to our fight plan? Where are the angles? Where's the jab? Where's my fighter? What the fuck is going on here? Where's Kid Coole? Where's Parnell Coole?

Billy's got wild curly white hair that's bald on top. He's got a big, beat-up nose that roams his face. His face gets red when he's upset. His face is very red.

—What have I told you? he asks his fighter as Kid sits on the wooden stool, getting his wind.

—What?—

—Jesus, Kid, I'm through fuckn around wid ya. Either get on board or get off the fuckn bus. Get off the fuckn pot. Stop waistn my fuckn time, for crissakes. You're gonna lose this fight if you don't come outta your trance.—

—Okay, Kid manages to say.

—No, no, Billy answers, jumping up and down, looking like he's going to have cardiac arrest. It's not okay. It's K.O. Either you knock this bumfuck out or it's all over.

—How?—

—What do I always say? he asks Mike White.

—What you say, Billy Farts?—

The bell is about to ring. Billy leans into Kid Coole, the scrawny little lightweight, and says

—I never back up unless it's to my advantage.—

The Kid is about to answer Billy, and the trainer shushes him. Billy Farts takes the mouthpiece from Mike White with his plastic-gloved hand. He places the mouthpiece into his fighter's mouth.

—Back up, he says, but make it to your advantage.

The bell rings, and it is such a relief for Kid to go back against the other guy. The opponent, Blue Rivers. No matter how much punishment the opponent delivers, Kid's glad to be in the center of the ring away from Billy Fart's angry red face and his glaring eyes and his shouting voice and his stinking breath.

—Back up, Kid hears Billy say, but only if it is to your advantage.

10.

Blue Rivers is overly aggressive, and he's had his way the entire fight. He bulls through Kid's jab and he whacks his sides with the gloves. His feet are fast enough that Kid is not able to counter.

Kid's face is red and swollen, and his dark eyes are puffy. His dark eyebrows are filled with clots of blood. His whole mouth is bleeding. His liver hurts. So do his kidneys. There is a pain behind his blurring eyes. His arms weigh a ton each, and it is nearly impossible to hold them up, to protect him from the blows or to throw a punch back at Blue Rivers.

Then it comes to him again, not as a thought in his head, but an idea in his muscles that Billy is right. Billy Faherty is always right. He is just that kind of guy, someone who it is worth listening to, especially as his advice might save Kid's life.

Blue Rivers steps toward Kid Coole, lunges really, and Kid steps back.

Kid counters with a hard right after planting his feet, and Blue Rivers crumples on the canvas, blood in his nostrils, spittle coming from his mouth, a bubble of blood, eyes rolled up in his head.

The bell rings.

Kid looks for his corner.

He sees Penny Half-Dog waving to him, waving him home.

He walks briskly to the corner.

11.

—STEP TO THE RIGHT! Step. That's it. Move to the right. THE RIGHT, KID! Plant. Plant your foot.

EXPLODE!

Get out of there. Get out. Don't get tagged. Get on your bicycle. Move. Circle. Circle. Jab. Jab.

DOUBLE JAB! YES! YES!

Kid, that is beautiful. Ain't that a thing a beauty, Mike White? Look at that jab. Now that's a jab. It ain't a jelly-donut punch. Look at the fuckn welt on the other guy's eyebrow. Look at that!

THAT'S A JAB!

What? No, no. Don't stand there.

What did I show ya? What did we do? We jab. We jab. We move. We bob and

weave. We stick and move. We move. Do the combination later. Now we stick and move.

STICK AND MOVE. THAT'S RIGHT!

That's my boy. You got yourself in the right rhythm, Kid. Don't stop. No goin' toe to toe. This ain't no
slugfest. This ain't no disco. Hey, Mikey. Mike White! This ain't no fuckn disco, right? We're gonna beat this guy with our heads. Hey, ref! Wake up!

DID YA SEE THAT LOW BLOW?

Did you see it? What are you, blind, ref? Why don'tcha become a baseball umpire? Jesus H. Christ, he stepped on my man's toe.

HEY, REF!

Defend yourself, Kid. These bastards don't have your best interest. This ref is Bluerivers' uncle. They're in fuckn cohoots. That's what they are—cohoots. Protect yourself at all times. Nice jab. Nice one again. Yes. Hook.

HOOK! GOOD!

I like it, Kid. I like it. A cross.

BEAUTIFUL!

Oh, my God, Mike White, did you see that uppercut the Kid threw? It lifted the other guy off his feet. A five-punch combo, Mikey, baby. Didya see the fuckn Kid? Fuck the ref. We'll K.O. the motherfucker. Mikey, Mikey. Get the stool. Get the spit bucket, Ralphie. No, no, whatshername.

Irene. Mary. Eileen. Deirdre.

Penny!
Goddamn Penny!
Penny Half-Dog!

You got the Endswell? You got the water? You got the sponge? Get ready. Count down. Sixteen. Fifteen. Move, move, Kid.

MOVE!

Take the round now. Plant. Stay, stay. Slip. Go under the clothesline. Yes! Ten, nine. Get the stool ready, Mikey. Mike White. Ready to go. One minute. No talking. I do all the talk. Let him rest. Give him some water. WATER! Good, good. Three-two-one. Bell. Okay, get the Endswell on his eyebrow. Don't want it opening up after he's fightin' so swell. Kid, kid!

KID!

Over here. Jesus.

JESUS!

We're wastin' precious time. Sit down! SIT! Listen, Kid!

LISTEN!

No, no,   LISTEN!
You're doing okay but you gotta move more. You gotta circle. Snap the jab. Be crisp. Snap it. Mikey, give the Kid some water. Breathe. BREATHE! That's it. Breathe. Spit into Ralphie's bucket. Into Penny Half-Dog's bucket. Spit into the fuckn bucket, Kid. Don't swallow that bloody shit. Now go out there. Do what I told ya to do. Move. Stick and move. Jab, jab. JAB! Then load up. Set it up with the jab. Then unload. Breathe, Kid, get your breath. Okay, we're ready to go. Get ready to go. Get ready...—

12.

Kid sits on the stool. It is made of wood. It feels good. It feels good to sit down and rest. He gets one minute. Which is almost up. Get his wind. Locate the stamina button. Push it. Get going, pal. Get some water. Man, is he thirsty. Do his bones ache. Does his chest feel a pain. Like a sucking wound. He can't suck enough oxygen into his lungs. This fucking guy. This Blue Rivers knows how to fight. But when a fighter is tired, in the middle rounds, the body tenderized by punches, he gets very sensitive. Suddenly the numbness leaves. The body loses its adrenaline rush. A fighter is left tired and sore. That's how Blue Rivers was starting to be. He had gone from being a very crisp, good fighter to being a tired one. He was no longer in the present. Blue was back in those early rounds that he had been winning. Suddenly Kid Coole was now the dominator. He was there. Kid is there.

Right there.

There.

Kid is there in the round.

13.

Kid jabs. He jabs. Jabbin' to the break of dawn. Then Kid Coole goes to the body.

Here's how it is done.

He jabs. He jabs. He moves. He looks for the right way there. He finds an angle. He sees an opening. He goes for it. He's looking for the body, but he pretends that he's head-hunting. After the jabs, Kid throws a left hook to the opponent's ear. It stings. How does he know? Kid sees Blue Rivers wince. Then Kid throws a right cross with all his weight behind it.

He has the other guy's attention.

Now it is time to become a body snatcher, time to pulverize the other human being. Take the mind and the body follows. Take the body and the fighter collapses.

Kid throws a right to the side of his opponent's body.

But he's really looking to use the left. He wants to deliver a ferocious hook to his opponent's liver.

When you land a well-placed punch on the liver, it feels good. At least, it feels good to the fighter who delivers it. Him? The other guy? Blue Rivers? Dude's hurting. Shmuck's in pain. No, no, other guy's in shock. The body goes into shock when it gets hit like that. The other guy's face looks like he's been electrocuted. His whole system has gone haywire. His body is being arrested. Blue Rivers winces badly.

It is at this point that Kid throws an uppercut. But first he needs to lower his center of gravity. He hunkers down. He throws the punch upward, letting his own body rise from the knees as the punch ascends skyward. The best place to land the uppercut is right under the jawline. But you want to hit the jawbone squarely.

Kid Coole lands an uppercut. You hear the jawbone dislocate, shatter and break.

The pain between the liver and the jawbone is excruciating.

Bell rings. End of round.

They go to their corners.

14.

Blue Rivers comes forward, lurching towards Kid Coole. Kid sets. He fuckn sets. He do what Billy Farts told him to do. Kid let dufus Blue throw the jab, slightly off balance, and Kid, he come underneath it. Kid come under Blue Rivers. Cometh the fire. Kid hits Blue the best shot of the night. The side of the body. Blue quivers. Blue shake like he got cerebral palsy. Like he Ali with the Parkinson's shake. Blue Rivers look like he got a bad case of shits. Kid follows up with an uppercut. He uppercut him. He cuts up the motherfucker. He cuts him. Slices him up the center with that punch. Kid truly uppercut the motherfucker good. He cut upward into the opponent's jaw. Blue Rivers seem cockeyed from it. The motherfucker be rocking on his feet, tipsy like an Irish wino in the alleyways of Sticks. Motherfucker be nearly out on his feet.

Blue Rivers try to wrap up Kid Coole.

Blue embrace the dude known as Kid Coole. He embrace him good.

But Kid Coole, smaller and stronger, rocks and bucks and fights his way out of this embrace.

If Blue Rivers holds on, he got himself a victory. He got himself a title shot somewhere down the line. Kid Coole got nothing but a lifetime of sparring sessions with ranked fighters.

Kid Coole fights and bucks and manages to throw a loopy left-hand punch, hooking it into his opponent.

The loopy-doopy left lands to cockeye the motherfucker Blue further.

Blue wobbles. He warbles. He waffles around.

Kid hit him a right.

There!

Kid goes downstairs.

Kid hits the motherfucker with two vicious body shots. But this fucking Blue Rivers just don't want to cooperate. Blue Rivers don't want to go down to the canvas and be counted out. It is like Blue Rivers got more will, more determination than Kid Coole do. Blue is going to last the round, win the fight by points.

But then Blue Rivers finally accepts the consequences of the two vicious body shots, and he collapses on the canvas. Like a pile of wood. Like a ton of bricks. Like a bag of shit.

Blue is center ring with his mouthpiece hanging out on his bloody lip.

This ain't what Billy Farts told Kid to do. But it was kosher. It was the only thing that Kid Coole could do given his situation. Kid could not put Blue Rivers away with an uppercut or a head shot. He put the motherfucker away with those two vicious body shots.

Kid stands in a neutral corner as the referee counts.

Blue's eyes are open but unfocused. His legs are spread apart. Like he was doing yoga stretches. The gloves rest on either side of him, like he was a tripod.

Blue ain't moving. So the ref counts him out.

15.

Kid Coole stalks around the ring, letting everyone know how tough he is. The crowd had not liked Kid's opponent, even though Blue Rivers was the local fighter. They had cheered Kid Coole. But now they boo Kid Coole, too. They boo him.

Billy Faherty, the trainer and manager, grabs his fighter and tells him to knock it off.

—A champeen never gloats, Billy Faherty says.

—Fuck you, Kid Coole answers.

Kid was going to gloat, to glower, to storm and strut and stalk around the ring until he was good and ready to leave. He would walk the walk, and talk the talk.

—There are other fighters besides you who have to use the ring, the referee says.

—Fuck you, Kid Coole tells him.

Kid would leave the ring when he was good and ready to leave the ring.

He was not ready to leave. He is not ready yet.

—You're being an asshole, Mike White says.

—Fuck you, Kid says again.

—Fuck me, Mike White says. You're the one being the asshole, Kid.

Mike White rarely said such things to Kid or anyone else. It was not Mike's style or manner to speak to another human being that way. But he's upset with his fighter, and he lets Kid Coole know how upset he is.

—Fuck everyone, Kid Coole says.

—It takes one to know one, Mike White tells him.

Then the adrenaline leaves Kid's body. He stands there exhausted, looking out at all the faces in the auditorium looking back at him. The faces have a malignant cast to them, edgy and fed up with his shenanigans.

The woman in the skimpy bikini bathing suit who walked around the ring holding a big card that listed what round was coming up walks over to Kid Coole and hooks her arm in his, and waltzes him out of there, doing in a few seconds what the ref, the trainer, the cutman, and the crowd could not accomplish for ten minutes.

People boo him.

Kid tries to walk away from the round-card girl in the bikini suit, but she pivots on her highheel and spins him around. He's impressed by her scientific mind, using a fulcrum to diminish his own power and strength. Kid asks her for a date.

—You got to be kidding, she says.

Once she has him out of the ring—and Mike White steps over and throws Kid's robe at him—she walks away. So Mike White says

—You'll catch your death of a cold if you don't put that robe on.—

He rubs Kid's shoulders as Billy Faherty leads his fighter from the ring area to the dressing room.

16.

In the dressing room, Kid sat on the rub-down table.

—You never want to make a spectacle of yourself, Billy said. That's how come those bozos out there were booing you. You never want to make a spectacle of yourself, Kid.

—Fuck you, Kid said.

—I'm beginning to think he's had too many fights, Billy said to his cutman, Mike White.

—He's all right, Mike White called back. The Kid's fine.

—I don't like a spectacle, Billy said. I train my fighters to be respectful of other people. That includes the referee, the judges, the round-card girl, the press, the paid admissions, the old fight crowd, and the opponent. Blue Rivers. He beat you once. He's the only guy in this whole fuckn universe who beat you fair and square once upon a time. Just remember that, sonny. Remember that I train people to carry themselves with dignity. Anyone can strut like that.

—Fuck you, Kid Coole sang.

—Fuck you, fuck me, fuck everybody. Pretty soon you can say fuck you to boxing. If you want to get a title shot, I would advise you to change your stinkn thinkn and your fuckn asshole tune, sonny.—

Billy Farts had his fighter's attention. Billy Farts said:

—Anger is not an emotion. It is an attitude hiding an emotion. Once the anger slips away, the cockiness goes with it. I taught you that. I have taught this young fighter, Mike, and I've taught him a lot of things that have nothing to do with fisticuffs. It's about human psychology. Anger only exhausts a fighter.—

Kid sat on the end of the rub-down table, hands at rest, legs dangling, and he felt helpless and bereft of his anger now. He felt alone and scared. He was exhausted, just like Billy Faherty said he would be from his anger. Kid cried.

—It's okay, Mike White said, patting his shoulder.

—We're fight people, Mike, we are in the warrior business, the violence business. We ain't pacifists.—

—Ali was pacifist.—

—But we're talking about Parnell Coole, Billy Farts said to Mike White. It's Parnell Coole who needs the attitude adjustment.

—Amen, Mike White said.

THE LATE ROUNDS

"Sometimes, I can't even remember my own name."
—Floyd Patterson

1.

Boxing was a game of inches. That's what Billy Farts said. He heard it from Whitey Bimstein, the legendary trainer. A fighter only had to move an inch to slip a punch. Step one inch to the right, and you are not where the other guy expects you to be. Then you are ready to do your own damage. The other guy is trying to figure out still where you are or where you went. At least that is what Kid Coole remembered Billy Faherty saying. Kid might have misunderstood his trainer. He remembered Billy saying: A fighter only has to move an inch to slip a punch. Well, even if Billy didn't say it, Kid remembered it that way, and that's how he put it into practice, that is what his muscles told him, what his bones said. Move an inch, slip a punch. Billy Farts also said that his fighters were every inch a king. He told them: I didn't learn that from Whitey Bimstein. I learned it from Shakespeare. Kill all the lawyers, Billy also said, and he also explained to Kid that he was once again quoting from William Shakespeare. Billy Farts was a classy guy. That's why Parnell Coole trained with him. It was Billy Faherty who came up with the name Kid. At first he wanted to call Parnell by the name Irish Kid Coole. Billy even wanted to get Kid to change his name legally to that, kind of like how the middleweight Marvin Hagler changed his own name to Marvelous Marvin Hagler. People then started to call Parnell by Billy's new name for him. Kid Coole. It stuck. And Kid liked it. But he didn't change it legally the way Marvelous Marvin had changed his own name. Kid was his nickname. His family still called him Parnell or Parnie. No one called Billy Faherty by his nickname—Billy Farts—at least not to his face. Billy had been around the block a few times, the old trainer liked to say. The trainer had been around boxing a long time, going back to his tutelage with people like Whitey Bimstein and later Cus D'Amato, before they had a falling out. That's how Billy Farts wound up upstate. Cus had dragged him along to Catskill, and then they had their famous falling out, and Billy had moved on to Sticks and Leathe, opening his two gyms and training fighters on his own. Nowadays he only talked about Whitey Bimstein. It was Whitey who told him that boxing was a game of inches. But it was Billy Faherty who said that his fighters were every inch kings. Parnell Coole was not yet a king. In order to be considered a king in Billy's world you had to be a serious contender, a champion or a ranked fighter, and Kid Coole was moments away from being any of those things. You are on a journey, Billy told him, and you are about to arrive at a place where you will become every inch a king. The journey had begun. That's what got Kid out of bed every morning before the sunrise. That's what got him to work, to the gym to work out, back home to eat properly and get enough sleep. Kid ran four or five miles nearly every day, rain or shine, hail or sleet or snow. He got up and went out, and he ran, he did his roadwork. He ran around Sticks, this little community on the Hudson River, deep in the Hudson Valley, midway between New York City and Albany, just across from Leathe and the Catskill Mountains. Every mile that Parnell ran he approached the status of those kingly inches Billy Farts spoke of. Every step moved Kid towards those royal inches. As he ran, he heard his trainer's voice urging him on. As Kid Coole ran, he threw punches through the cold night air, the steam of his breath pouring out of his nostrils and mouth. He threw real punches at imaginary adversaries, and every once in awhile, he would stop, throw a five-punch combination, dance around sideways, slipping imaginary counterpunches by an inch, by a hair's breath, by kingly degrees.

2.

Kid sat in Gladiola's living room, watching the fights on television. Antonio Goya was fighting Lutrec Spears. Both lived in Miami now. Goya was Dominican. Spears, Haitian. The fight was boring because they neutralized each other, and it made it a hard fight to call. But Kid usually could tell when something was about to happen.

An accumulation of punches in a certain place of the body suggested that events were about to change.

A constant tirade of left hooks by Lutrec to Antonio's liver told Kid that Antonio was about to lower his right elbow to protect the sore liver. The fighter did lower his right to protect the liver. Thus a chain of events was set in motion.

Instead of protecting his temple and jaw with his right hand held high by the ear, Antonio dropped his guard to help the sore liver.

Lutrec jabbed at the head. Then he unloaded a big left hook there. He hooked again.

When Antonio raised his hand, Lutrec pounded the sore liver.

It was the liver shot which dropped Antonio to one knee. He claimed a slip. His corner said that the canvas was wet. Their fighter slipped. They asked the referee to mop up that part of the ring. The referee told Antonio's corner to shut up.

The fight went on.

Antonio lowered his hands to help the hurt liver. Lutrec unleashed a stiff jab, followed by a left hook to the head. Then came a big right and Antonio went down.

He rested on his knees. He was trying to find his equilibrium. But he was counted out while still on his knees.

—Who won? Gladiola asked, coming into the living room.

—I'm going to be fighting Lutrec Spears for the lightweight championship.—

—Mozel tov, she said, matter-of-factly.

—The fight will be made in a few days. But I'll have many months to prepare.—

—You're gonna fight that nigger?—

—He ain't a nigger.—

—Then what is he, boy?—

—He's from Haiti.—

—And Haiti don't have no niggers?—

—I don't like that word.—

—Cause you ain't a nigger, that's how come. But since I am a nigger, it's all right with me.—

—I'm fightn him soon.—

—The nigger?—

—Lutrec Spears.—

—Lordy, she said.

—Yeah, I'm real happy 'bout it.—

—You don't look real happy.—

—On the inside, I'm real happy.—

—Well, you coulda fooled me, boy. You look like your usual miserable useless self, Kid.—

—No, I'm real happy to be alive.—

3.

After the fight Gladiola asked Kid to cook his healthy bowl. It consisted of tofu, vegetables (broccoli, string beans, carrots, sprouts), and brown rice. He cooked it in sesame oil with miso and soy sauce. There was garlic, some ginger, a scallion, and he cooked the brown rice in chicken broth. He learned to cook it from Sunny, Mrs. Kim, from the plastics factory down by the river.

As they ate Kerry came into the kitchen.

She flopped down in a chair. Her legs spread across the linoleum floor. Her body took up more space than it needed.

Kerry wore sandals, even though it was freezing outside. (Snow was expected shortly.) She also had on huge, baggy bell-bottom jeans, and a psychedelic halter top that showed her new tattoo that surrounded her navel piercing.

—Mom, she said, I need some advice.

The day before she told her mother:

—I don't need any advice from you, loser.—

—I'm on the pill, the daughter said.

—Great, her mother answered.

—And I had sex already with a guy.—

Suddenly neither Gladiola nor Kid were eating.

—Gary, Kerry said.

—Gary?—

—He's my new boyfriend.—

—Gary's twenty-one, Gladiola said.

—Twenty-three, mom.—

—He's too old for you, her mother told her. You're only fifteen.

—Almost sixteen, daughter corrected mother.

—Sex! Gladiola screamed.

—Well, it's better than using drugs, right, ma? And I'm on the pill. I can't get pregnant and wind up a teenage bride like you were.—

Gladiola looked to Kid for help. But his role was not clear. He was a friend of the family. Half the time the daughter was flirting with him. The other half the mother was.

—Your mother will have good advice, he said to Kerry finally. Listen to her.

Kerry looked at Kid like he was a gnat. Then she focused on her mother.

—I have a problem, Kerry said.

—I'll say you have a problem, her mother responded.

—No, no, ma, I mean I got a *mechanical* problem.—

Kid could tell from the look on Gladiola's face that she did not know what a mechanical problem was. Neither did he. When he fought the wrong way, threw a punch awkwardly or stood in a way that threw off his balance, his trainer Billy or the co-trainer Mike would tell him that he had a mechanical problem. That was a good problem for a fighter, he figured, but maybe not for a daughter. A mechanical problem was fixable. It was not like having a poor spirit, lack of courage, or even lack of natural ability. You could correct a mechanical problem, he thought. Unless Kerry meant a carburetor or a distributor cap problem, then he was lost.

—I'm dry, Kerry said.

—Dry? her mother asked.

—I can't get moist inside.—

—What? Gladiola shouted.

—I'm not wet enough, Kerry said. It hurts.

—You shouldn't even be fucking, Gladiola said. You're fuckn fifteen!—

—Almost sixteen.—

Out of nowhere—why, he didn't know—Kid said—

—Have you ever heard of foreplay?—

—Foreplay?—

Both of them looked at him. Their eyes flashed at him. Gladiola's eyes were too wide. Kerry's looked confused. Now her mother seemed to look angrily at Kid. Their faces softened all at once. The room changed its pressure. They breathed.

—He's right, Gladiola found herself saying. You need foreplay to get wet.

Then:

—Christ, why am I telling you this fuckn information?—

—Foreplay? Kerry asked.

—Your boyfriend needs to kiss you. He needs to play with you. You know. Downstairs.—

—Downstairs?—

—He needs to manipulate your clitoris.—

—Mom, Kerry said. I'm fifteen years old. What's a clitoris?

Kid stood and said he had to go home.

—Sit down, Gladiola said, then shoved him back into his chair.

Then to her daughter:

—A clitoris? It's right here.—

She pulled down her running shorts and showed Kerry.

—If you rub it gently it becomes aroused.—

—Oh, I've done that since I was a kid, Kerry said.

Then Gladiola went back to being a mother. She pulled up her shorts and sat down.

—Gary's too old for you, she said, once again. Find a boyfriend your own age.

—Wasn't Dad twenty-three when he knocked you up? she asked.

—So?—

—And you were even younger than me, Kerry said.

—Yeah, her mother answered, and I'd be the first to admit that I made a lot of mistakes.

—Like having me?—

—You are not a mistake, Gladiola said. You're the love of my life, sweetie.

Kid stood to go once again and slipped on the kitchen tiles. It felt like a knockdown. He got up from the floor. He said that he had to go home.

—Sit down, Gladiola ordered him.

—Sit, Kerry echoed her mother.

He sat down in a chair at the kitchen table.

—I want to talk to Gary about this, Gladiola said.

—It's a free country, Kerry told her.

Kerry went back to sprawling in her chair. Her legs reached out over the linoleum floor. She slouched. The big tattoo around her belly button and her pierced navel filled the room. She popped a bubble with her gum.

From being a woman moments ago, Kerry went back to being a young girl, even a little girl.

Gladiola went back to being a very old thirty-year-old mother. Her hair was in corn-rows. She wore black nylon running shorts and sneakers. Her top was yellow. It was made of a synthetic fabric. The material was hi-tec. It moved sweat from the body to the outside of the shirt. Her presence filled up the kitchen.

—I want to talk to Gary, Gladiola said.

—I can't stop you, Kerry answered.

Her mother picked up the telephone to dial.

Once again, Kid stood to leave. Kerry pushed him back

into the kitchen chair. He had no balance. He fell back down.

His mouth was very dry. He needed to stay hydrated. He needed to sleep early. Run before sunrise. He thought:

I am not the husband. Not the father. I am an occasional boyfriend. One of many. Among men and women. I am a friend. I have to start going to the gym. I am going to fight Lutrec Spears for the lightweight championship of the world in two months' time. I am not a father or a lover. I am not a boyfriend. I am a friend. I hardly know these people. They have their own problems to solve. I have mine. I need to work on my combinations. I need to work on my lateral movement, my eye/hand coordination, my foot speed. I need to get my twitch muscles fired up for action. I need to go home and sleep. What I know, they don't know. I know how to fight. I don't know anything about teenage daughters; I don't know anything about girlfriends. I'm a fighter. I know how to fight. I need to go home to sleep. I need to get some sleep. I need to sleep.

4.

Kid sat on the porch at the nursing home next to his Aunt Ella.

—You don't like when I squeeze your hand, she said.

—I don't care if you squeeze my hand, Kid said.

—Gimme, she said.

Aunt Ella took his hand and held it, tightening her grip gradually. Kid quickly pulled it away.

—See, she said.

—What?—

—You don't like.—

—I like, he said. I like.

He gave her back his hand. But she only patted it now. She knew. He did not like when she held it tight. It was her brother Tony who told her. He said that fighters didn't like to have their hands held tightly. They made their living with their hands. Maybe it was the one delicate thing about being a fighter; they did not like to be squeezed. They liked a soft handshake.

Kid gave his Aunt Ella a kiss.

He had gone from Sticks to Leathe and then taken the bus to her nursing home on the Hudson River next to the cement plant that barfed out its black sooty smoke. Aunt Ella had become frailer, fully there in her mind and spirit, but her body was fading away.

—I love you, she said.

—You too, he said.

—Me too what?—

—I love you, Aunt Ella.—

—Commere, commere.—

As he approached her, she pushed him away.

—Get outta here!—

Then she did it again.

—Commere, commere. Then: Get outta here!

—You're nuts, he said.

—No, you're nuts, I'm crazy. Speaking of which, how's Tony?—

—He's okay.—

—Liar.—

—He's old too.—

—Too?—

—You're old. He's old.—

—Thanks a lot, pal.—

—Even I'm gettin' old, he said.

—You're a kid, Kid.—

Aunt Ella laughed.

You're a kid, Kid.

—Fighters age different than other people, she said.

—True, he said. They do.

—You're okay, she said.

—I'm gettin' better fights. Billy's movin' me to bigger events.—

—You really go to see Tony? she asked.

—I see him.—

—When?—

—Once a week, he said.

—You saw him this week?—

—No.—

—Last week?—

—No.—

—What the fuck, Kid.—

—When I have time, I go to see him. He's okay. I mean he's nuts. You know that already. But he's all right in the way Uncle Tony is all right.—

She understood.

—Commere.—

—Don't start that shit.—

—Hey, God don't make shit.—

—I come over there and then you tell me to get away from you.—

—It's a fuckn joke.—

—Ha, ha—

—Ha, ha, hearty-ha-ha—

—I got to go, he said. You all right?

—I'm not all right. I'm old and I'm dyin'.—

—But you're okay, right?—

—What the fuck, you got wax in ya ears?—

—You're okay, he said. I can see you're all right.

—Jesus, she said, I got one foot and two armpits in the grave.

—I gotta go, he said.

—You just got here.—

—I just got here, he said, but I also got to go.

Aunt Ella knew he was only coming for a short visit, to bring her a few items she wanted, and to leave. He had dropped off the tissues for her nose, the warm socks, the mittens, the knitted hat, the newspapers and magazines she couldn't find at the home. It really was time to go. He had to catch a bus to take him back to Leathe, and then he had to figure out a way to get home from Leathe to Sticks. Maybe someone at Billy's gym would give him a ride home. Maybe Mike White or Penny Half-Dog.

Fighting was a shitty business. It was a dirty, shitty business. But in this part of the world people did all sorts of things to make money, including dirty, shitty things. They worked with hazardous waste, in cement kilns that burnt garbage for fuel; they worked as steeplejacks on skyscrapers. They farmed, working from before sunrise to after sunset. Housewives trundled the kids off to school, then worked as porn stars on the Internet in order to pay bills. That was dirty business, too. Boxing, he figured, was no more dirty than any of those jobs.

Aunt Ella came out of her silence, and patted his hand.

—You're a good boy, she said.

The Kid was not wild like other people in his family. That's why Aunt Ella liked him.

The Kid leaned down to kiss her goodbye, and she pulled him down toward her, giving him a big, wet kiss on the lips. She slapped his cheek lightly.

—*Il mio bambino*, she said. You're a good boy, sonny.

He said goodbye to Aunt Ella and he left the porch and walked down the path to the parking lot where he would wait for the bus to Leathe.

The bus pulled in, opened its door, and he got on. As it drove away, he could taste her lipstick on his lips, and still smell her perfume in his nostrils.

5.

Kid got off the bus in Leathe, then waited for another one that took him back to Sticks. He got off the bus in Sticks on the side of town near the hospital, and should have walked the fifteen minutes back to his room. But instead of going home when he got off the bus, he walked down a side street where the freight train tracks ran through Sticks. Suddenly he found himself face to face with the tall, bald man with the shamrock tattooed on his big neck. He wore the long black leather coat that was shaped like a cowboy's duster, and under the coat he wore a tight black tee shirt, tight-fitting jeans, and high black boots that reached almost to his knees.

An enormous fawn-colored pit bull was straining a lead which Shamrock held in his right hand. The dog was so powerful that Shamrock had to do all he could to keep the dog in place as it growled and menaced Parnell Coole.

—St. Vito, St. Vito, St. Vito, Kid prayed to the patron saint of protection from wild animals.

—We got some business to settle, Shamrock said. On my command, this dog is going to tear you limb from limb. But first I want to let you know what a mistake you made bothering me that morning in the alley. My business is my business, you little shit. Who the hell are you to tell me what I can or cannot do? Who are you to challenge me? I defy you to explain why you would throw a punch at me. You don't even know who I am.

The pit bull growled and bared its teeth. Its pointy tail was tucked between its rear legs, and the dog hunkered down, as if to prepare for battle.

Then Kid saw movement in the shadows of the alley. It was Gladiola, wearing a black down coat and a wool cap, jeans and winter boots. She looked like a thousand other people in Sticks.

189

—He's all right, she said, nodding towards Parnell Coole.

—Who the hell are you?—

—That don't matter a goddamn who I am, Gladiola said. Who I am is none of your fucking business, fathead.

Then out of her down coat Gladiola pulled out a small automatic pistol, and pointed it at the man.

—You ain't gonna shoot me 'cause you don't even know who I am.—

—You raped my fifteen year old daughter, she said matter-of-factly, still pointing the gun at the man.

—Put that gun away, Shamrock said, without a quaver in his voice, looking her firmly in the eye.

—I'll shoot your fucking dog, Gladiola said, changing her focus.

She pointed the gun at the ferocious pit bull that lunged at her from its lead. She closed her eyes and shot the gun, hitting the dog squarely in its head, just between its eyes, and slightly upward on its forehead. A tiny hole opened up in the dog's forehead, then exploded back through its brains, and exited the back of the head, spraying blood everywhere.

Shamrock's leather coat was covered with the blood and brains from the dog's head, and the dog lay quivering on the ground, its eyes blank and pitiless near the snowy ground.

—Why'd you do that? Shamrock asked.

Gladiola pointed the gun at the large, bald-headed man with the green shamrock tattooed on his neck.

—I'm in no mood for your lip, she said. Don't fuck with me.

—That was the best pit bull I ever had, Shamrock said, not speaking to Gladiola, but to the universe at large.

Shamrock kneeled in the snow and pulled the lifeless dog towards him.

—He was my best dog, Shamrock said.

He kneeled in the snow with his dog and he cried.

Gladiola grabbed Kid's hand, and together they ran down the alley, then weaved from street to alley, and back to street. Near the river, she told him to go ahead to the Locomotive, a bar in the center of Sticks, and she would meet him there. She was going to throw the gun into the Hudson River. Kid said he would wait for her, but she urged him to go on. She would meet him at the Locomotive.

6.

Kid stepped into The Locomotive bar off Harding.

Kid was not a drinker like his brothers or his mother or father. He did not like the taste of beer, wine, or whiskey. He did not understand the rituals of drinking. The last time he had had a drink was years ago. He forgot what it tasted like. Forgot what it did to him. Everything came undone inside of him.

The progression was an old family one. He took a drink. The drink took a drink.

Then the drink took him.

Kid stood at the bar, looking at himself looking at himself in the mirror. He thought:

It comes from the feet. Then it travels up the calves into the thighs. At the center of gravity which is known as the crack of your ass the torque pulls it in another direction up the spine, along the back muscles. It rotates into the cuff of the shoulder. Traveling from the biceps, it rolls through the forearm where it meets the wrist. Which is where it joins the fist, moving forward into an overhand right, a straight punch to the other guy's jawbone, nose, or forehead.

Power gives and power takes. All power to God, the Almighty Savior, the One who makes it all possible. No God but the One God. Power to Him. Power to Me. Power to You. Power to Everyone.

Kid wished all life were as easy as it was in the ring. He liked the rhythm of things in there.

—Protect yourself at all times, the referee said.

But Kid was powerless over so many things. This drink, for instance. He could feel that he was no longer Parnell Coole but some other piece of human machinery—some piece of human misery. He was powerless over Gladiola shooting the dog or even Shamrock kneeling in the snow, holding his dead dog, the big man crying. None of these things had anything to do with Parnell Coole who was just a by-stander, a witness. He had no other role in all that business.

—People, places, and things, his trainer Billy Faherty said.

Billy being the recovering alcoholic, he liked to bring that into the training sessions. He believed that winning was about spiritual connections, not physical ones.

—Let go, Billy Faherty said. Bend like a branch in the wind. Flow like water. Turn and flow. Don't go toe to toe unless you're going to trick the other guy. The other guy goes toe to toe, Billy said, you put him in a trance. Let him think you're there for keeps. Then take one step, right or left, it don't matter to me. Take a step. Create a new angle, a new perspective.

Kid looked at himself in the mirror behind the bar. He ordered a beer. Then he ordered another. He drank a bottle of beer and asked for another. Then he drank that beer and had another. What did Billy Farts say the progression was? Oh, yes: you take a drink, the drink takes a drink, and then the drink takes you. How many was that? Fuck it, Kid thought, who's counting? I ain't. What's it matter. Fuck it. I'll let the drink take another, then I'll let the drink take me. What did it matter?

He looked at himself in the mirror behind the bar. His face was clean, well-defined, chiseled, his cheekbones prominent, his nose twisted, his eyebrows full of ruts and imperfections. His bald head had nicks and cuts throughout. He smiled like an idiot back at himself.

Where was Gladiola? Should he go out to look for her? But then she told him not to leave the Locomotive until she got there, so he had another beer and another one after that.

He felt tipsy, then he felt himself drifting away from his own body. He was elsewhere from where he was. He looked at the blur of his face in the mirror behind the bar.

Other customers stood there talking to one another, but no one came over to say hello to him. They did not know him. He did not hang around such places. He was not familiar with the easy way that people spoke about sports and the local news, the politicians in Washington and the world.

7.

I'm not pushy. I'm easygoing. I live a simple life. I don't need much. I live in one room. Everything I own I could fit into one, beat-up suitcase that my Aunt Ella gave me years ago. (I got to call her; she's not well. She told me that her brother, Bushy Gilhooley was not well either. I got to go visit him at the fireman's home.) The rest of the stuff—all my boxing gear—I keep in a duffle bag. I don't own any art. I don't even have CDs, just a portable radio and tapes. No television. TV makes too much noise in my head. No fancy suits or shoes. Boxing shoes for the gym. My boxing shoes, my boxing gear, tape, wraps, jockstrap, shorts, sleeveless shirts, socks. I got a pair of cross-trainers I use for walking around. Running shoes for roadwork. Work boots for work—the Red Wings.

Mrs. Kim, my boss's wife at the factory, made me buy a pair of Red Wing boots. It's her favorite brand. So I bought them. They are good workboots, very comfortable on my feet, and warm and dry.

I also have a pair of black loafers.

I got some gold chains and a gold watch and a gold bracelet and a pinky ring, and I also have a TAG sports watch with a rotating bezel so I can time my runs in the morning.

I got one fancy pair of slacks. A sports coat. One tie, a Nicole Miller that a sportswriter gave me. It has a boxing motif, gloves and ticket stubs from fights. I have a couple shirts. Some nice Italian sport shirts. Underwear. Socks.

I got a little Buddha. A photo of Archie Moore with three of my oldest brothers standing around him. The old man met Archie down the piers and arranged the photo op.

I got a one-volume encyclopedia. A dictionary. A short story collection. Some essays. A book of poems a brother wrote. I got a little blue notebook that same brother gave me.

—Write your thoughts in it, Mickey Mack said.

—I ain't got no thoughts.—

—Whatever comes into your head, he said. Words, phrases, feelings you have. Remember how I taught you about the memory palace.

—Oh, yeah, the memory palace.—

Kid wanted to tell his brother that his feelings were in his body, not his mind. He told his brother that he had no words, no pictures, no ideas, nothing in his mind. His mind was blank. His head was empty.

8.

—That's it, the bartender told him. You've had enough.

Kid had just asked him for another beer.

195

—What?—

—Finish up and let's go, buddy.—

Kid picked up a beer bottle and threw it through the mirror behind the bar. The bartender, twice his size, ran around the bar and grabbed him and tried to wrestle him to the floor, but Kid squirmed out of his grasp. He pulled the man's shirt over his head, and then hit him five or six times on the side of his stomach, until the fellow collapsed. Two more fairly big men jumped on him. He knocked out one of them, but he hurt his knuckles doing it, and he managed to hit the other guy with a straight right.

He was cut himself, maybe from a beer bottle, and blood streamed over his face.

9.

When he came out of the blackout, he was at the top of the Headless Horseman Bridge that joined Sticks to Leathe. But he wasn't on the walkway. He was hundreds of feet above the traffic lanes on the bridge, and hundreds more feet above the mighty Hudson, balancing on a steel girder. He had climbed up one of these steel girders to the pinnacle of the bridge. At the very top of the bridge, red warning lights blinked on and off several feet from where he stood. The wind ripped into his face and even through his gloves and his jacket. The bridge loomed up over the river, and he saw the water running past underneath, hundreds of feet below. He thought of jumping, but then decided he wanted one more drink before going to his end. He came down off the girders, walked back into Sticks, and went back to the Locomotive. He asked for another beer. But the bartender refused to serve him one. So Kid left.

By the time he got to the door of the house where he rented a room, the police were outside, and they arrested him. He spent the night in the Sticks jail, in isolation. The next morning he was arraigned, and a lawyer whom Billy Faherty knew represented him. The lawyer got it thrown out as long as Kid made restitution to the bar owner and agreed to go to AA meetings.

Parnell Coole was sent to after-care at a halfway house on Muhammed Ali Way. His counselor made him keep a journal. Kid was not allowed to fight the match that would have put him in the championship bout. As a result of being arrested, he was removed as one of the fighters in the championship round.

—Consequences, Billy Farts said. You are responsible for your actions in and outside the ring. Now you've got three-thousand bucks worth of damages to pay. You threw some chairs, broke some windows, smashed a table, destroyed an antique mirror behind the bar. The next thing you know you are not a boxer but a jailbird. But you're lucky, Billy said. The judge sends you to A.A. for 90 days. Now there's one serious problem you have to deal with. The Boxing Commissioner has suspended you pending the outcome of your rehabilitation, so you can't fight Lutrec Spears for the lightweight title. My advice to you is a simple one, Parnell Coole.

—Surrender, Billy said. It means coming over to the winning side. Look it up in the dictionary if you don't believe me.

—I believe you, Kid said.

—Look it up if you don't believe me. Either you surrender or you won't be fighting again.—

Kid owned an American Heritage dictionary, and he looked up words all the time. Surrender did not mean coming over to the winning side. It meant giving up control because of a compulsion.

So Parnell Coole went to a meeting because he wanted to give up control of his compulsion and put the matter in the hands of some authority greater than himself. At least that is what Billy Farts told him to do, and what Billy said Kid Coole listened to.

The woman who ran the meeting said:

—Court slips will be signed after the Lord's Prayer.—

That night Kid looked up the word power in the dictionary. It was the ability to act effectively. To exercise control. Forcefulness. He put down the dictionary next to his bed.

10.

The Kid swooshed the mop back and forth over the elementary school floor. The children came out of their classrooms. Most ignored him, didn't even see him there. Janitor was a forgettable character. Quiet. Trembly. He seemed to talk to himself under his own breath. He was small and dark and silent mostly. Not creepy. Not scary. He was nothing. A blank. This empty shell in the hallway, mopping the floors or cleaning the toilets in the lavatories or washing windows and or doing errands. He didn't drink and didn't smoke and instead of doing roadwork, he walked everywhere when he wasn't working as a janitor at the school or an orderly at the firemen's home or putting palettes of plastic transparencies onto a truck for the Kims. When he couldn't find regular work, he worked for the antiques people on Harding Avenue. He was hard-working and quiet, never a bit of trouble from him. He lived in the rooming house, in the back of the big white house on Poe Street, down the alleyway, and up the back stairs. He was neat and silent, empty-headed and harmless.

Children teased him, but he ignored them.

He was sort of good-natured. He said so little. No one could remember hearing his voice. Did he even say two words?

He was dark and silent.

Small.

Not frail, not skinny.

Just small. Compact, maybe. He did not look strong. Everything about him was a deception. He did not appear to have a muscle in his body, and yet he was incredibly strong. His strength coiled inside of him.

One day he lifted a desk by himself, carrying it across the room for the nun. Another time he pushed the car out of the snow for the monsignor. He pushed the car by himself.

Some children made fun of him or teased him. But some of the children got the thought into their heads that it was not a good idea to tease the custodian.

—Hey, champ, a young boy called out.

Kid smiled.

He had not been taking care of his teeth. One or two were missing in the front. His smile was not pretty. It was crooked and dark across his dark face. His hair was short, and his head was nearly bald. His skull glistened in the lights of the hallway of the school. His arms were tight and hard and simple.

The boy who called him Champ wore the school uniform of brown pants, shoes, and socks; tan shirt; and green tie with the school insignia SAS.

—Hey, the janitor said to the young boy.

—The boy's friend said, Hey, chump!

But Kid Coole did not hear him because he was involved in mopping the floor. Maybe he was listening to that funny music in his head. What do they call it? Oh, yeah, the music of the spheres, only with a boxer it was more like the music of the crazy brains, scrambled and gooey and not working the way they worked for other people.

He said aloud, but under his breath,

—I need to finish before Mother Superior comes by. But already I am too late—

because the nun who scared the Bejaesus out of everyone came stomping down the hall, her shoes clicking, her rosary beads clanging, her starchy habit whispering Evil Evil Evil.

Mother Superior inspected lockers, walls, and floors.

She was a fearful woman to everyone, including Kid Coole. But luckily she did not even notice the janitor because some boys were fooling around down the hall.

—No horse-play in the halls! she called out.

The noisy hallway turned to silence.

Kid Coole mopped.

Mop-mop, he said. But not aloud. To himself. He said, Mop-mop. Then aloud:

—Moppety mop mop—

When he finished mopping, he had to wash windows. Twelve big windows in every classroom. Eight classrooms in all. He would be washing windows until late at night. He heard that there might be a job in the plastics factory down by the river again sometime soon. It paid better than being a custodian in a Catholic primary school. Maybe he'd go there on his day off and speak with the Kims. They always liked him a lot. Didn't Mr. Kim use to let him off when he was fighting? Didn't he even come to some of the Kid's local matches and cheer him on. Mr. Kim was an awfully nice guy. So was Mrs. Kim. She used to make him a lunch of rice and beancurd and seaweed and sesame seeds, soy sauce and hot mustard.

—I like the way the plastics factory smells, he said to no one in particular, especially since the hallway was empty now that the Mother Superior had cleared it of children.

After Mother Superior left and the students went into their classrooms, Kid found an empty room to begin the window washing. As he dipped the cloth in the soapy water, he said to himself, not to himself but aloud,

—Move to the right! Move to the right!—

—We live by such small degrees, Billy Faherty once told him.

One survives by such subtleties of action. An inch here. An inch there. Everything was an angle. Move. Move. To the right. To the right.

—Move to the right! he heard Billy Faherty shouting, and Ralph Half-Dog pounding the canvas in the corner to direct him into it, and old Mike White standing there with his bucket of ice and Endswell and the tools of his trade as assistant trainer to Billy Faherty, his lifetime partner in the cornerman business.

The Kid moved to the next window.

11.

Finally Kid went back to the gym, hitting the heavy bag. Billy Faherty came over.

He watched Kid throw punches at the bag, but said nothing for a long time.

—Fear is good, Billy finally declared. It just depends what you're gonna do with fear. Cus used to tell us that. Fear is your friend in the ring. He once told me that he didn't want to work with anyone who didn't have any fear. I agree. You got to have some fear. It just depends what you are going to do with it. Are you gonna let it rule you or are you gonna let it help you, make you a better person?

—And power? Kid asks.

—You're a lightweight, his trainer said. Power is not your game, Kid. It's not everything. Did Barney Ross have power? Did Benny Leonard? Benny Leonard was as smart as Sigmund Freud. But he was a boxer, not a psychiatrist. I prefer an athlete with some brains. I like stealth, slyness, never back up unless it is to your advantage. That's what I like. I like to work with someone who uses his head. Who thinks on his feet. I like a fighter that's flexible. Inflexibility is a sign of mental weakness. It's a sign of mental illness, too. And power? Power? You can get done in by your own power. It creates a false impression in your mind, Kid. An illusion. When I look into a fighter's eyes, I want to see clarity, order, enthusiasm. I want a guy with a head on his shoulders. Give me Benny Leonard over Sonny Liston. Give me Ali over Ernie Shavers. Quickness and quick-mindedness over pure strength. Hell, George Foreman had one of the biggest punches of all time. But he couldn't beat Ali in Zaire. Why? He was not flexible. He could not bend, Kid. His power created an illusion for him, and he believed the illusion. It told him that he was invulnerable. No one could stop him. Instead of will power, give me willingness. Give me a mind quick in the open field, Kid. Even Roberto Duran was much smarter than he was tough. But sometimes he was too smart for his own good. You got to be humble. Humility isn't being small. It's being right-sized. You're a lightweight. You need to move quickly. Stick and move. Jab, jab. Then go. You need to think like a brain surgeon out there, Kid. You're not strong enough to be dumb. But that might be the best thing about you.

Mike White came out of the office to tell Billy Faherty that he had a telephone call.

The lecture ended.

Kid Coole went to the locker room to shower.

ROUND TEN

1.

Kid walked through Times Square. Earlier in the day, he had sparred with this up-and-coming welterweight in Brooklyn. A Spanish guy. Named Carlos. He forgot his last name. Short-term memory. He had dinner in Little Italy. Some people knew who he was and wished him well in his upcoming fights.—Let's hope it's at the Garden, one of them said, against Lutrec Spears.—Then he came uptown to see a movie. He was tired and felt good. He walked north toward the park. He had money in his pocket and he hadn't been hit much. Not too much anyhow. No cuts on his face. No lumps on the body. A couple of tiny bruises, here and there. But you get used to that. It was part of the business. Goes with the territory. His sparring partners were plenty tough. Billy and Mike wanted him sparring away from Sticks and Leathe, down in the City. They wanted him to get used to the distractions. The media attention. The night-life. The hustle-bustle. Also, they wanted Kid sparring with quality partners, up-and-comers themselves. Different weight classes. Different angles. Speeds. Kid liked sparring in Brooklyn. He had been born in Brooklyn, in Bedford-Stuyvesant, St. Mary's hospital, like all his brothers and sisters. Even though he hadn't grown up there, he liked Brooklyn.

The movie was good. But he couldn't remember what it

was about or who was in it. He thought it was either Diesel or Denzel. His memory sucked, but even before boxing it was not very good. He remembered things from long ago. Stuff that just happened was harder to conjure. But he did remember that the movie was a futuristic job. Super-heroes. Too bad life didn't have any of them. There were lots of special effects. The actors stood there, and looked good. They probably made a lot of money. A lot more than the Kid got for his own line of work, which didn't even pay his rent and electrical bill.

No matter what the universe threw at them, the actors looked good. Their clothes were clean. Their hair was neat. Not that he worried about his own clothes or hair. He dressed simply. A nylon gym outfit, cross-trainers, good socks (only a hole in one toe). A few gold chains, a gold ring with a black stone and a small diamond, a gold wrist watch. He wore a Kangol hat backwards. Bad-ass. He shaved his head once a week. But he wished life were as simple as the movies. If the world threw something at you and if you didn't duck, you would get hit in the face. Protect yourself at all times, the ref said. Don't lead with your chin or drop your guard, his trainer Billy Faherty told him.

He walked north through Times Square, and around Fiftieth Street he remembered that Jack Dempsey had a restaurant here. At least that was what Billy told him. The Kid was too young to know who Hurricane Jackson was much less Jack Dempsey. He watched DVDs of all the great fighters, and that's how he knew who they were, their styles, their flaws, their peculiarities, and strengths.

Then Kid crossed the street, and there he was. The Champ. Not Dempsey. The King. The Greatest. That's what they called him, and they were right. He was the greatest.

The Champ no longer shouted.

—I am the Greatest!—

His movements were slow, and he shook.

Poor guy.

The Kid said to himself, I'll never get like that. I'll get out before it is too late. Billy Faherty always says you only have so many fights in you, and once you reach the limit, it is time to get out.

He stood in a crowd of about one hundred people, shouting and calling to the Champ. No one noticed the Kid because he was small and quiet and dark. He blended right into the crowd, part of the scenery of Times Square.

The Champ—the frail, human, broken, fallen champeen—waved to them. Then he surprised everyone. He did the famous shuffle. Only slo-mo. Champ started to spar with different people in the crowd, and people all around were hooting and hollering and laughing. You could feel his good will toward them. He was like a god still. You could still see the good looks under the fallen features, the stumbling legs, the hunched shoulders, the puffy cheeks and the swollen eyes.

The Champ went up to a toddler in her mother's arms and he pretended to spar with the baby.

His handlers, his bodyguards, his entourage, they all looked on, used to the Champ still acting for everyone. The crowd was silent except when they let out a roar of laughter.

Like now. He did a magic trick which had everyone shouting and hollering at him, waving in his direction. Then the crowd got silent again as the Champ moved among them, like a pope dispensing blessings.

The Champ shook all over.

Yet you could tell it was still him. You could tell by how he balanced himself. They say that the legs are the first thing to go and the punch is the last. But Billy Faherty taught the Kid something else. His trainer told him that the old timers—the great old ones from the past—had something else besides legs and punching power.

—Balance, Billy Faherty said.

—Balance? The Kid asked.

—Balance, he said again.

Even with the shakes, you could see the Champ still had great balance. Some might call it grace. But Billy once said that

—grace is only part of it—

The Champ moved through the crowd as gracefully as a ballerina.

He still had that great rhythm of a champion, even if it was slow. The rhythm was very sure of itself. He was the Champ. That's what his rhythm seemed to convey. He was the Champ, and they were his subjects. They were his court. He was the Greatest. They were just who they were, and nothing more. But he was the Greatest. The King of the World!

The Kid had a brother who was just a couple of years younger than the Champ. His brother had been a rising young middleweight, knocking out people, moving right along. He knocked out ten people in his first twelve fights. The brother was training in that beat-up, upstairs gym on Fourteenth Street. It was the gym run by Old Man before he moved upstate across the river in Leathe from where the Kid lived in Sticks.

The Kid's older brother was sparring one afternoon, and Sugar Ray Robinson walked in. He was at the end of his career. After watching the Kid's brother spar a few minutes, Robbie comes over to him, and he says

—All right—

That's all he says.

—All right—

Sugar Ray kind of whispered it, the way old fighters talked, like all the words in the head had been boxed out of them.

After you've had two-hundred-and-forty fights, what good are words?

—Kid, his brother said, Walker Smith, a.k.a. Sugar Ray Robinson, was the greatest fighter of all time. I modeled my style on all the great fighters from the forties and fifties. Guys like Jake and Rocky—the two Rockies—Irish Billy, the Mongoose, who was one of my personal favorites. Carmine and Gene, and Willie. Sugar Ray was my idol, man. I tried to model my whole style after his on account I was a middle, almost six feet, okay, five-eleven and three-quarters—same height as Iron Mike—and I was long and seemed thin like Sugar Ray was. Having Sugar Ray say—all right—was not just all right, it was like a dream.

Then the Kid's brother was in the Fourteenth Street gym run by the Old Man, and who should be there but Himself. The Champ. The Greatest. The King of the World! Only they did not call him the Greatest yet. He was the Olympic champion. He was not even the Champ yet. He had won a gold medal in the Olympics, and had had a couple of professional fights. The only person who thought he was the Greatest was himself. He was knocking out people everywhere. He was kicking ass and taking names later. He'd let God sort it out. He was the number one contender.

The Kid's older brother used to say that you could see faster people than Sugar Ray. But they were in the lighter divisions, and they didn't have his power. And there weren't too many of them—no matter how light they were—who were that much faster than Sugar Ray. You could see bigger punchers in the heavyweights. The Brown Bomber had a punch like a thousand-pound sledge hammer. What Sugar Ray had was that he was just about as fast as any lightweight and he had a heavyweight punch, even if he was a middleweight. It was hard to find anyone finer than Sugar Ray.

Then there was the Greatest. The future Champ.

The Kid's brother saw the future Champ in that gym downtown. Older brother told the Kid that he had never seen a heavyweight so fast. But he also never saw a heavyweight so athletic and graceful.

—He had balance like you would not believe, his brother said.

—The Champ was like a ballerina, Billy Farts once said, only he had that wicked jab and killer right.

His brother concurred.

—The Champ was as fast—and slick—as Sugar Ray. He also seemed to have a punch like Rocky or Brown Bomber, the two great heavies.—

Kid's brother could aspire. He aspired to be like Sugar Ray. He might never get there, but it was within the realm of possibility, of a clear fantasy. But as he stood in the gym on Fourteenth Street, there was another kind of fighter in front of him. The future Champ. The Greatest. The King of the World! The Kid's brother was supposed to be really fast with his hands. He could land a five-punch combination, lickety-split. But the Greatest was something else entirely. He was big. Deceptively big. He didn't look big from across the other side of the gym or even across the ring. But up close he was really a heavyweight, only built like a middleweight. And he could move. He moved like Sugar Ray, only in a bigger package. He moved like a great middleweight, only he was a heavy. And punches? The Champ could throw two or three times the number of punches of the Kid's brother in the same amount of time. How did he know? His brother told him. His brother had seen it close up, right there in the gym downtown.

His brother quit boxing that very day. He went off to the state teachers college in central New York, the one that was across the river and into the mountains and clear across to the middle of the state.

2.

The Champ worked the crowd like it was the old days. The Kid had never seen a human being instigate so much love and human warmth. He could feel the energy all around the Champ. He could see what his brother meant when he said

—the guy fuckn baffled me—

Grace and balance and dignity and rhythm, and even unsteady in his gait, he looked you right in the eye. Looked into you, deep down into you. He put his hand inside of you and grabbed you by the soul. He shook. He moved. He shook again.

The Kid could tell how hard it would be to beat this guy in his prime. You sensed that kind of thing in another fighter, that unknown ingredient.

Everyone was in his corner.

Plus, he was much bigger than you realized. He was not a pumped up light-heavy the way Spinks or Foster or even Marciano or Mr. Patterson were. The way Evander was. This was a genuine heavyweight. Big bones. Thick limbs. Barrel-chested, broad-necked, wide-shouldered, ham-fisted, long-legged. Wide-hands, round-wristed. This was the real deal. A great lightweight fighter did not stand a chance next to such a human force.

The Champ plunged deeper into the crowd in Times Square, and his handlers seemed worried that he was going too far, getting too far out of their sight. They were paid to watch after him, make sure he was all right. He could fall. Have a seizure. Fall down dead.

3.

The Greatest stood in front of the Kid.

He raised his hands to spar and snap a jab at the Kid's head. The Kid slipped it. The Champ threw another, and the Kid ducked. Then the Champ faked a jab and came overhead with a big right which he held at the last second. But it didn't matter because the Kid already slipped him.

The Kid was a lightweight, small and quick.

—All right, the Greatest whispered. All right.

They shook hands. They did it the way fighters shook hands, very softly, very respectfully of the other's tool. He asked the Kid his name. The Kid told him

—I'm Kid Coole—

The Champ's voice was only a faint whisper, but he said,

—Kid Coole, huh?—

—Yeah, the Kid said, I'm Kid Coole.

The Kid figured that if he said his name twice, the Champ would remember it.

—You cool all right, Champ whispered. You real cute, too.

Then he pulled the Kid off his feet, mugging for the crowd. Everyone was laughing and shouting and applauding him. The Champ fed off them. He mugged some more. He pulled the Kid to his chest and looked real menacing at the Kid.

—Well, Kid, he said, whispering, I'm The Greatest.

After The Champ dropped the Kid, he drifted away, almost as quickly as he sparred with the unknown lightweight from upstate New York in the town of Sticks, a Hudson River backwater, but now a Brooklyn-trained contender, and another face in the Times Square crowd, just another anonymous admirer. Maybe Kid Coole was going to be the next lightweight champion of the world. Now the King of the World was gone. He'd already gone back into the throng in Times Square, leaving Kid Coole in the back of the crowd. Kid was just another boxer one fight away from a championship.

The Greatest gave and received their love.

People applauded the Champ.

The Kid could see that the Champ was exhausted. His aids helped him to a limo. It was almost like that James Brown routine when he was so exhausted by his performance that a band member assisted The Hardest-Working-Man-in-Show-Business off the stage. Then James Brown came back, throwing off his cape, grabbing the microphone, singing like there was no tomorrow.

But instead of bursting back out of the limousine like James Brown, the Champ got into his limo with the blacked-out windows and he drove off into the night.

The Greatest never returned. He was gone for good, and the people drifted back into their lives, going off in different directions from Times Square.

—All right, Kid Coole said. All right.

The Kid whispered it as he drifted northward toward Central Park, and a long walk through it to God's knows where for the night.

—I'm cool, he laughed. I'm Kid Coole. I'm not as fast

as Sugar Ray or as powerful as the Champ. But I'm tough enough.

That's what Billy Faherty always told him.

—You're tough enough, he said.

He was. He is. Kid Coole's tough enough.

The Kid walked northward, now up Broadway, past Columbus Circle, Lincoln Centre, Needle Park, Eighty-sixth Street, Ninety-sixth, One-hundred-and-tenth. One of his brothers would let him stay the night, and the next day he'd go back to Sticks, up on the Hudson, upstate, and train with Billy and Mike for his big fight shortly. Kid remembered what his trainer Billy Faherty had told him a few days earlier in Sticks.

—The next one is your big one, Billy Farts said.

4.

—Auntie, he said, calling her at the other nursing home.

—Yeah, she said, tired and grouchy.

—Uncle Tony...—

—What?—

—He...—

Kid started to cry.

—Did he pass? she asked.

—He died, Kid said.

He cried again.

—That's okay, she said. It's all right. He doesn't have to suffer no more.

—And you?—

—And me?—

—Are you gonna suffer?—

—I'm like Sylvester the Cat, she said. All my life's Sufferin' Succotash.

5.

A small man is never a threat. He cannot intimidate the way a big man can. What a small man can be is quick. Kid is that. Stinging. Yes, that, too. Irritating. Yeah. Relentless. True. A good small man is no match for a good big man. But a good small man is able to wear down almost anyone but a big man if you let the small one hang around too long. That's Kid Coole.

But he also has a knockout punch. At least, on occasion, he has knocked out people. Not all at once. It was one at a time. He knocked them out fight by fight, not round by round. Nearly always it was deep into the fight when he had been quick, stinging, irritating, relentless, and Kid wore them down.

A big man might step into the ring and put the fear of God in an opponent. When Kid looked at tapes of Sonny Liston, he saw that maybe Sonny was that kind of fighter. Mike Tyson was that way early on in his career.

Kid Coole weighed one-hundred-and-thirty-five pounds. A lightweight. He was five feet five inches tall. He'd never had a muscular build. But he was wiry. He was not the toughest of guys. Not even a tough guy. He'd do terrible in a tough-man competition. He was not that strong, not that fast. But he was fast enough. He was strong enough. Kid's quick. Kid's resilient.

So he was not a tough guy. But he was tough enough.

What he had was stamina. Plus he was very stubborn. He had the will to win. He believed that he might topple buildings and collapse mountains with his will power. You'd have to kill him to beat him in a fight. He had a tremendous resistance. Kid was quiet but he also was intense. Though he was a good defensive fighter, he was also good on offense. He never gave up.

His weakness?

His teeth were terrible and always costing him money. It seemed that every time he saved a little money, a dentist came along and took it away from him, doing surgery, pulling teeth, making bridges or plates. Ultimately it would weaken his jawbone considerably.

He went to a periodontist because his gums were swollen and bleeding. He thought maybe it was the new mouthpiece he had made. But the mouthpiece was fine.

So the hygienist gave them a deep cleaning. As she scraped and talked to him, pressing his head into her chest as she moved here and there to scrape and then evacuate the spit, water, and blood, he began to think that all his relationships with women had disintegrated, including those he had with Gladiola and Kerry. He liked the hygienist's voice. Her manner.

Her name was Della. That was what her nameplate said.

Della. She was small and cute. Dirty blonde hair. She wore a dental smock of pastel green. Also, she had on matching pants, and she wore white leather sneakers.

Her dirty blonde hair was short. She was small and muscular. Beautiful teeth. Really nice pearly smile. Lovely green eyes. Must be Irish. At least a Kelt. Hell, she could be North Italian for all he knew. He realized he knew nothing about women. He knew nothing about anyone. He was a fighter, plain and simple. He had no skills outside the ring. He lacked charm, social skills, even a vocabulary to communicate.

But he asked her out.

She said, yes.

—Yes, she said. I'd like that, Kid.

—Great, he said.

What did she see in him? he wondered or even what did he see in her? Where would he take her if she wanted to come back to his place, that little, dingy room in the boarding house? He hadn't cleaned his room in weeks. Hadn't washed the sheets or made the bed or done his laundry. It smelled like a gym.

But she said yes and the next night he took her out for a pizza. They were going to see a movie on Route 9, but it was sold out.

She said,

—Let's go to my place to watch a video.—

He nodded okay.

They drove in her car because he didn't have one. He had a license, but he didn't own a car to drive. She asked if he drank ever. He said no. Then he amended that. One night, recently, he drank, and got into trouble. He punched holes in a wall. He punched out a bartender. He hit some patrons. He broke some glass. Broke a mirror. Then he had climbed to the top of the Headless Horseman Bridge, joining Sticks to Leathe across the river. Police came. He went to jail. Did he leave anything out? Did it matter?

—That's okay, she said.

But it wasn't okay. He still had to go to AA meetings, and he was delayed in having his championship fight against Lutrec Spears.

—Have you heard of Lutrec Spears?—

—No, she said.

He explained who the Haitian fighter was.

—Well, good luck, she said.

—Thanks.—

Then she drove to her place outside of Sticks. A string of new linked townhouses in an old cornfield. Each townhouse had two bedrooms, a garage for the car, living room and dining room and kitchen.

She parked the car in the garage and they entered the townhouse through the kitchen door in the garage. He sat at her kitchen table, sipping a gingerale she handed him.

—I find all of this intriguing, she said. Your life. Not drinking. Your next fight.

—Yeah, he said.

—I find you a fascinating person, Kid.—

—Yeah.—

—You're a good listener. Well, I'm a talker, she said. But

you already know that from me doing a deep-scrape on your gums.

Della leaned over to him and gave him a kiss and he responded back to her kiss. They moved to the couch. Kissing some more. Embracing.

—Good, he said.

—Very good, she said.

—I'm good with my hands, he says again.

—You're a boxer, she answered. You better fuckn be good with your hands, man.

—Well, yeah.—

—You're not good with your feet?—

They sat on the couch at first. Now they lay on it, side by side, with Della slightly on top of him. The television played in the background. A movie. A video. And the stereo played in the background to the television. Something jazzy, moody, easy and light. They sat up.

—I've got good foot work, he told her.

Her legs were tucked under her buttocks. She looked really good on her couch. Small and compact, no fat, no nonessentials. Her smile big and pearly white.

—What's the difference between roadwork and jogging?—

—Jogging you do to get in shape, he said.

But he was winging it. So he went on.

—Roadwork you do after you're in shape and need to get in fighting shape.—

Della asked how much he slept because she had read an article about how much sleep fighters got.

—I sleep seven hours straight at night, he said, from nine to four in the morning. Then I get up and do my roadwork. I run for about forty minutes to an hour. I get home, take a shower, go back to sleep for a couple more hours. In the middle of the day I take a nap, sometimes for an hour, sometimes longer. Then I take another nap in the evening.—

—Before you go to bed?—

—Yeah. Like I said, I like to sleep.—

After he told her this, Della leaned over and kissed him.

—Your arm and neck are likes rocks.—

—I'm in good shape, he admitted, and then she unzipped his pants, pulled them down, and began to lick a bead of sweat that dripped down his abdominal muscles and into his crotch and then took hold of his cock and put it in her mouth.

—Oral hygiene, he said.

She laughed and then choked.

—I thought you weren't into talking, she said. Don't make me laugh, Kid.

—Sorry, he said.

But then she sat up, rubbed her mouth, removed pubic hair.

—You want to go into the bedroom?—

—Yeah, he said.

—Oral hygiene, she said. That was very funny. I have to remember that. I'm going to tell Doctor Ross that one on Monday.

—Hey, I'm a funny guy, he said.

—You really are, Kid. You surprise me.—

They made love.

Afterward, lying in the bed, under the covers, she said,

—I'm falling for you.—

But he didn't say anything.

—Cat got your tongue?—

He began to cry.

—What's wrong? she asked.

But there was nothing wrong.

—I'm crazy, he said.

Maybe it was from being hit so much. Or it could be from his genes. Kid came from a crazy family. So he'd been hit on the head too much. Now he was laughing. Then crying again.

—Crazy love, she said, laughing, too.

—Yeah.—

6.

One cool morning when the colors were electric in the trees and the sky, he took the urn with his uncle's ashes and walked to the river a few blocks away.

The river was tidal, and the tide was high. Steam rose out of the water, like fog, only the sky was clear and Kid saw the Catskill Mountains looming up in the distance on the other side of the river behind the city of Leathe. The mountains were red and yellow and tinged a light purple.

Never leave your wounded behind, Kid thought.

That's what a Marine captain had told Parnell Coole when he came to collect Uncle Tony's body from the home. His uncle had been a fighter, too, and won twenty-seven fights, eighteen by knockout, and was undefeated before going into the military. Six years later, four of them as a prisoner of war, Uncle Tony came home a broken man. He worked as a caddy on a golf course for awhile. He drifted around. Eventually Kid got him into the home just outside of Sticks, and that's where Tony stayed until he died. Once in awhile, Kid visited him there. Then he would report to Aunt Ella about her broken-down brother. Always Kid lied, saying Uncle Tony looked good. But Uncle Tony never looked good. He was a drooly, empty, broken man.

Parnell opened the urn and let Uncle Bushy's ashes catch the wind and drift down to the water. When this was finished, Kid tossed the urn in a public garbage bin and trotted down one of the alleys all the way to the other side of town a mile away.

He ran down the main street to the river, a mile away. Turned around, and ran up another alley. Kid did this for five or six miles. Going from alley to main street, up and down, east to west, west to east.

Afterward, Kid walked around. He kept asking himself why he was born and why he was here and what was it he was supposed to do.

BETWEEN ROUNDS
(ONE-MINUTE IN THE CORNER)

III.

My head was full of flickerin black light and my head full of black lights, flickerin, I told my/self later, you shd have seen it comin, every/one saw it but you, the angles, the deception, the sly tip/toein, pitty/pat of those graceful feet, the dreamy sweet nuffinks, every/thing one big fix, you big shmuck, the cornermen shoutin. How cd you not see it comin? the roundhouse to the head, the short body punches, hard and painful, to the liver. The heart punch stopped yr heart from its beatin. His two/punch combination to the head stopped you from ever thinkin again, friend.

ROUND ELEVEN

1.

Gladiola and Kerry were fighting again. They fought all the time lately. It started with words and escalated to shouts. Sometimes the daughter threw things at her mother—glasses and plates, knick-knacks and cups and anything that wasn't nailed down.

A glass broke. Gladiola's face was cut. Blood was everywhere.

Kerry ran out of the house. Kid found her later, after taking Gladiola to the hospital and back home after she was stitched up. He got on his bicycle and went looking for that wild child everywhere.

She sat in a little park overlooking the river where all the local teens went to drink beer and smoke dope.

—I hate her, Kerry said.

He put his arm around her.

—Your mother is a good person, he said, and she's had a hard life. But she loves you and she does the best she can for you. She wants only the best for you.

—Crap, she said, and a can of cliches. That's all you talk, Kid. You don't have real thoughts in your head. What's in your head?

—Slogans, he said.

—No joke, she said. I don't even think you have slogans there.

Then Kerry changed course. Kerry cried out,

—She sucks, and I hope she dies.—

—Your mother is a good person, he said again.

—So was Adolf Hitler a good person.—

—No, he wasn't, Kid said.

—Why not?—

—He killed all the Jews.—

—Jews never did nothing for you.—

—I don't know about that.—

—You gonna tell me that Jesus was a Jew.—

—He was.—

—Fuck off, she said.

—Okay, he said, and stood.

He started to walk away.

—Wait.—

—She's a hick, Kerry said as she and Kid walked down Harding Street. She's unsophisticated. I think she's illiterate, too. Mom don't have a brain in her thick, stupid head, Kerry cried, and she's as dumb as shit. Just like you, Kid.

—I'm not dumb, Kid said. I know how to duck when punched at, and I'm still fast on my feet.

—You're one of the dumbest fucks in the fuckn universe, Kid. You make Rocky Balboa look like a genius.—

2.

—Do you remember when everyone lived at home? his sister Eileen asked.

He did not.

—Remember the old house? Mary Grace added.

But Kid could not.

Samantha said that her own memory was fuzzy. She said it was because of drugs and alcohol. A lifetime of it. Sam was more than thirty years older than Kid. She was the oldest sister.

Oona told them that she remembered everything. She remembered being in the womb, she said, and she remembered her birth and her early childhood. She remembered being eighteen years old, leaving home to join a cult in Brooklyn. From Henry Street she went to the Ganges. Once she moved to India it was a short jump to marrying a swami. Her son Krishna was the offspring of that union. It was because of the meningitis he had as a child growing up in an ashram in India that he was deaf and going blind now.

Mary Grace declared that Kid had no memory because of fighting. But Deirdre observed that Kid never spoke much as a kid. Paddy and Kid and Junior and Frankie were the only ones not given to talking. Their family was nothing if not talkers.

Eileen said that Kid's memory should be deficient from concussive blows to his head. Eileen liked to use phrases like "concussive blows to the head" to impress everyone about her mind-powers.

—But the Kid is a great defensive fighter, she said. I've seen him fight. He's hard to hit.

His sister knew him like a book. He was a master of

deception, nothing more. He looked skinny but really was thick in the neck and arms and legs. He looked dark but was really pale. He appeared to be a weakling and in fact was a tough guy.

—Right? she asked.

Kid smiled.

—Yeah, he said, laughing.

3.

You only have so many fights. Once you reach the limit, you give up. You get out. You find another life. The problem Kid had was knowing when he'd reached his limit. You win a fight, like he did against Blue Rivers, and yet you come away a bit older, not your belly-button age, but an old man in this young body. Is it here? Is it now? Did I miss it a year ago? Kid worked a line of business where it was hard to know when it was time to go. He figured he had a few more fights left in him. But maybe he only had one or two more.

His old man Jackie Ducks, when he was still alive, once told Kid that his son was good enough to get himself killed. Kid knew what old Jackie Ducks meant. Billy Faherty told him the same thing when they first met and as recently as a few weeks ago.

—You're just good enough to get yourself killed, he said, echoing Kid's father.

Right now Kid had a couple of loose screws in his head. If he kept getting hit, he was going to wake up one morning and discover that there was nothing left in his head.

Already Kid had bad headaches.

Migraines.

When he got a migraine he couldn't stand light and noise. He lay in a dark room for hours or days until it went away. He didn't listen to music, he couldn't talk when the migraines struck. He got a nauseous feeling in his stomach. Sometimes he threw up. His head rung. One side of his head ached.

It hurt like it was punched hard by a good left hook.

Kid also had sinus problems. The cavities above his eyebrows and just above his cheekbones filled up with liquid.

He had trouble focusing or paying attention. It was distracting.

Other problems included money. He didn't have any. Prestige: his self-esteem sucked. Relationships: He had no honey. He'd see prostitutes in the city. But a prostitute wasn't a relationship. Even Kid knew that. He had women friends. But he wasn't sure if they really wanted to be with him. There was Gladiola. There was Kerry. There was that dancer in Atlantic City. There was the hygienist lately.

—Her name, he said, wondering.

It was all there, only it worked like an old hard-drive, slowly but determinedly.

Kid kept wondering what he was going to do when all of this ended.

Would he continue as he was? That included living in a single-room-occupancy in Sticks. Working at the plastics factory. He could mop floors at the Catholic school or be an orderly at the fireman's home outside of Sticks. The possibilities were endless, and yet limited to almost nothing.

He would see family once in a while in the City.

Once he stopped fighting, that would be it. He didn't want to be a trainer, a ref, a judge, a cornerman, or a mentor to young fighters.

He didn't smoke or drink.

Well, mostly Kid didn't smoke or drink. He still had probation for the bust-up in the bar. He still had to go to alcohol counseling. He still had to check in with a social worker every couple of weeks.

If he could win a big fight, he'd smoke a cigar. He'd drink a glass of champagne. After a recent sparring session, he showered, got dressed, and left the gym.

He stood on the subway platform, waiting for a train. He wore a dark nylon workout suit with a white stripe down the arms and the legs. He wore new white running shoes. He had a scarf around his neck to keep warm, and a watchman's cap pulled tight over his skull and ears. He wore his eyeglasses because lately his eyesight had been going. The glasses sat crookedly on his big, broken nose.

A group of kids walked over.

One said,

—You lookin' at me?—

Kid didn't answer.

—You deaf?—

—Who you lookin' at? the ringleader asked.

Still Kid didn't say anything. He was a ring-fighter. He

was not like his brothers. He was not a street-fighter. He was not interested in trouble. Kid didn't think of himself as a tough guy. He remembered what Billy Faherty always said:

—You're just tough enough.—

But also:

—When in doubt, Billy added, get on your bicycle. Run. Move. Scatta! Get out of there!

—What's your problem? a third one of the kids asked.

It was late. Kid should have left the gym long ago. But he stayed talking to people. He was lonely and he wanted to see family and he thought one of his brothers was going to show up at the gym and they would go for a meal together in downtown Brooklyn. His brother was a deep thinker. He liked to talk, too. This was a result of his accident. He nearly died in a fire. Now he was philosophical about it. He was writing a book.

—I got no problem, Kid finally said to the punks near the subway station.

—Who asked you?—

—No one.—

—You're my problem, the ringleader said.

—Cut out his pockets, one of the punks said.

That's when Kid Coole ran.

He was not fast but he was quick. He could run a sprint. But he was best over the long haul. He had more stamina than brute strength. His twitch muscles were very fast. Outside the ring, he had nothing to prove. He didn't even approve of fighting outside the ring. So he ran away from them.

They chased him for a block or two outside the subway station, but then gave up. Kid walked ten blocks to the next subway station, paid, got on, and took the subway to Penn Station.

He caught an Amtrak north to Sticks.

As the train rattled alongside the Hudson, Kid looked out at the dark night. He imagined the river. It was out there, sometimes deep, sometimes shallow. It was always flowing. Sometimes it flowed south. Sometimes north. It was that kind of river. It's a river that is not really even a river. His own life was like that. Because he boxed for a living, it was presumed that he was a street fighter like some of his brothers. But he was not. Like the river, he bent. He flowed. He moved along.

He sat back in his seat on the train and looked out the window, trying to see the estuary through the darkness. He barely saw its surface, reflecting light. He inhaled. Exhaled. He breathed deeply. What was their problem back there at the subway in Brooklyn? Then he remembered. Oh, yeah. It was me. I was their problem. They did not like me. They wanted to do me harm. But they did not know that I make a point of staying out of harm's way. Some people like to mix it up. I am not that kind of person.

His own problem was more complex than the street punks's problem which was with him. Let Kid put it in a nutshell. Do I fight two more times and hang up my jockstrap? Do I keep fighting? Maybe do ten more fights. Do I keep fighting until I am an empty shell? I am tired. It is late. He closed his eyes. He stretched out. He was small, though. If he stretched out, he was still in no one's way. The conductor would not ask him to pull in his big feet because someone might trip on them. He told himself everything was fine. It was fine. But Kid tasted something in his mouth—on his tongue. It was fear. He tasted the fear like it was an after-taste from a bad meal. He smelled anger, too. The anger rose inside of him, ugly and hot. Now he wanted to go back to Brooklyn and kill those punks. But, instead, he closed his eyes. He breathed. Inhaled. Exhaled. Deeply. Kid thought about his next fight. He thought about life after boxing.

—Perhaps I'll become a gardener.—

Then he laughed.

Kid laughed for the first time in a long time.

It made him wonder about his Aunt Ella. She was the only person who made him laugh. But he had not seen her for awhile. He wondered how Aunt Ella was as he drifted off to sleep on the train.

4.

Kid slept on the couch after falling asleep while the late-night news was still on. The two of them—Gladiola and Kerry—were in the kitchen arguing again.

Kerry told her mother that Gladiola was worthless. An embarrassment.

—You're a 'ho', mommy.—

—I ain't no 'ho', no how.—

—You fuck anything that walks.—

—'Ho's charge money.—

—You're a dumb-fuck 'ho', who don't know no better than to do it for free. You are an economic catastrophe, mommy.—

The daughter had gotten her eyebrow, nose, lip, tongue, stomach, and the lip of her vagina pierced and studded.

—You got more tattoos than the tattooed lady at the circus, Kerry said to her mother, and you're telling me about a couple of piercings.—

Then Kerry stood and walked away, right as her mother was going to talk.

Kerry went to her bedroom on the ground floor in the back of the house. She smoked pot and thought of calling a motorcycle gang member to whack her mother. Maybe kill that worthless scumbag boxer sleeping on the couch, too. But instead of calling the motorcycle guy to whack her mother and Kid Coole, Kerry fell asleep from the pot.

5.

Deirdre flew into Miami from the rain forest in Brazil. That's where she lived with her husband Jiao and the kids. Oona and Sam lived in Florida, one near Tampa, the other north of Miami. They met at the Miami airport and flew to New York. They had all come together for the birthday party.

Eileen was thirty-five years old. This was her birthday

party. Sam rented a conference room at the Ramada Inn near Kennedy Airport.

None of the brothers—other than Parnell—had shown yet. Quite a few of their brothers had said they would come to the party. No spouses or boyfriends were at the Ramada, except Mary Grace's boyfriend, Tony Bones, a legitimate businessman from Bensonhurst.

Tony wanted to talk to Kid about one of his friends in Brooklyn handling his career. Tony said he knew how to fix Kid's situation with the Commission. Tony could get Parnell reinstated. Kid was not interested.

—Billy Faherty is my manager and trainer, and Mike White is my assistant trainer and cutman. Ralph Half-Dog is spit-bucket. Well, Penny Half-Dog these days. Until Ralphie gets better.—

—Penny Half-Dog. What the fuck kind of name is that? And Billy Farty, Bill Farts, Tony Bones said. What the hell kind of name is Farty? Is that a real name? Does he fart a lot? What does he do for you, Kid?

Then:

—Having Billy as manager and trainer is a conflict of interest, Tony said. The New York State Boxing Commission will frown upon this innocent behavior once you become a champeen of the world. Billy Farty is in no position to represent you and train you at the highest levels of the sport. This requires professionals.

—Billy is a professional.—

—I mean people who know how to handle money and events. People who have contacts. People who understand contracts. People who know other people who know other people. The wheel turns. My people would not let you lose a fight to some bum in Utica, New York.

—Schenectady, Kid said. Billy believed in me when no one else did. Now it is my turn to repay the favor.

—Please, please, please, Tony Bones said, gesturing wildly with his lit cigar. Let's not get sentimental. We're talking business not romance. Loyalty is great. But you're missing paydays. Your career is slipping away because of your loyalty to Billy Farty who, with all due respect, I honor as a trainer, Kid, but as a manager? Come on. As a manager Billy Farty has his head up his ass. If you had a real manager, you'd be the lightweight champeen of the world today, not this fighter at the end of his career, sipping Coca-Cola at his sister's birthday party in Queens.

Tony had his opinion. Kid had his own. But you couldn't argue fine points with a guy like Tony Bones.

Mary Grace announced that she and Tony Bones were engaged. Everyone oohed and ahhed. They kissed her on the cheeks. They congratulated her. Kid tried to shake Tony's hand. Instead, Tony gave Kid a bear hug. Then he shook Kid's hand by squeezing it too hard.

Kid pulled it away.

—Jesus, Kid, you shake hands like a dead fish, Tony Bones said.

—I'm shy about people squeezing my hands, Parnell said.

—You guys are all nuts, Tony said, laughing.

Mary Grace came over and flapped her arms around Tony's big shoulders.

—He's my fiancé now, she said, kissing Tony.

Kid could tell that she liked saying the word *fiancé*. She stopped calling him Tony or her boyfriend. He was her *fiancé*. Mary Grace would not call her fiancé Tony Bones even when he introduced himself that way.

—Hi, he said, I'm Tony Bones.

—My fiancé, she added. Anthony Puglia.

6.

The other guy was awkward. He faked a jab. Kid doubled up. Kid came over it, counterpunching. But the other guy was waiting for him. Other guy threw a big right.

It hit Kid on the top of the head, to the right, near his temple. Kid was out on his feet. As soon as the other guy landed the big hit, Kid reeled backwards.

His legs got rubbery, and he felt like puking. Kid had no idea where he was, but he knew he was in some kind of survival mode. He tried to clear his head. But he couldn't shake it. Instead, he got on his bicycle, circling the ring and his opponent. Kid knew he couldn't win the round. All he wanted to do was survive it.

Kid backpedaled.

Then he juked right and left.

Nothing fancy, he told himself. You will be lucky if you get out of this round alive. Keep it simple, stupid, Kid said. Well, he didn't really say anything. No words were in his head. Only this funny music.

Fortunately, the other guy, Tyrone Brighella, a Marine from Quantico, was not a seasoned fighter. He didn't know how to put Kid Coole away.

When you get knocked out or take a heavy blow to the head, the commission suspends your license for 90 days. You have to have a brain scan to see if the rhythms of your brain aren't off. Kid hated being slid into the scanner. It was like being on an alien spaceship. He got claustrophobic. But he'd had several of them by now. Usually they sent him to a place on the Upper East Side in Manhattan.

Going back to New York, Kid was beaten up and swollen. His head hurt like you would not believe. It felt like he fractured his skull. Like an ax was planted there. He couldn't believe that the judges awarded him the decision. He hadn't earned it. He didn't deserve it. But a win was a win.

The crazy music in his head would play a different tune. The rhythm of his feet will match the beat of his gloves.

7.

Kerry woke to a crashing sound. She figured that it was her mother drunk or maybe one of her mother's drunken boyfriends. Kid was deep in sleep on the couch, but even he woke up from it. He got up and headed toward the back of the house, but could not figure what was going on.

The noise came from Kerry's room in the back of the house behind the kitchen. Kid figured that one of her wild boyfriend's was freaking out from crack or ecstasy. Behind the door, Kid heard snorts and cries, he heard Kerry screaming wildly, but the door was locked, and he couldn't get inside her room immediately.

—Mom, mom, Kerry cried. Mommy!

Kid broke open the door with his shoulder.

A deer had jumped through the bedroom window. Now it bucked and ran, knocking over dresser and chairs, breaking a mirror, sending CDs and a player flying.

Gladiola came running into the bedroom only to face the bloody, crazed, scared, injured deer.

—Help me, mom, her daughter pleaded because she was pinned in a corner, naked except for a blanket which she held up to protect herself from the rampaging deer.

Gladiola ripped the blanket violently from her daughter's hands, came up behind the deer, and she tossed the blanket over its head.

Quickly she tied the blanket securely over the deer's head, and the animal seemed to calm down.

—Open the fuckn door, she shouted at Kid, motioning toward the downstairs bathroom.

Kerry's mother lead the animal into the bathroom, talking gently to it the whole time, not letting go of the beast.

—Call the police, Gladiola said.

Kid did.

Kerry put on some clothes.

When the police arrived, she showed them where the animal was. Her mother had it near the tub, still talking to it gently. Kid stood next to Gladiola, watching this with dumbfounded awe. He was not really a country person despite all the years he had spent in Sticks and Leathe.

The deer was calm now as Gladiola talked to it.

A vet eventually arrived and sedated the animal, and then lead it away.

One police officer told Kerry how lucky she was to have such a cool mother who knew what to do with a wild animal in the house.

—Hey, Kid, another cop said.

—Hey, he answered.

—Any fights comn up?—

—Yeah, I got somethn somewhere, he said, desultorily.

8.

—Do you remember when mom stopped drinking? Deirdre asked her brother Parnie.

—My memory isn't good, he said.

He recalled a pivot he made that allowed him to slip a punch and then counter with a punch of his own. He didn't remember towns where he fought or fighters he got in the ring with. He remembered jabs. Hooks and crosses. He remembered a knockout in Troy. Then another knockout in Troy two weeks after that. He remembered a K.O. in Rome, New York. Two weeks later he knocked out someone in Utica. Then Syracuse. Kid would always remember Schenectady.

He had memory in his muscles and bones, through his skin and throughout the network of his veins. His memory snaked through his body in the lymph or it clustered in his limbic system, at the brain pan, in the back of his head and down his neck into his spine. The memory lived in his blood. Memory pumped through the body, blood to bone, bone to muscle, muscle to ligaments. This was what that body of memory told him:

—We come from a big family on Long Island. My mother was a beautiful woman. Our father was a difficult man, especially if you were one of his sons. My sisters remember an entirely different person than the sons remember.—

Strange how the body of memory had a voice almost like his own.

—I got in trouble when I was young and I was sent upstate. It was not a reformatory. Mr. Patterson helped to get me into a special school for troubled kids.—

Parnell stayed in the mountains.

When he retired, Kid would get a condo in Atlantic City. He'd walk on the boardwalk. See Whatshername, the dancer. Remember the feathers in her dance. Remember Pee-Aye. Remember the floor show. Maybe Kid would remember the old days. It was not important. He'd rather have good health than memory. The body of memory wanted wellness more than details, health and heartiness rather than knots of dendrons filled with names of labels on cans, cereal boxes, people's names, the names of the living, the names of the dead.

For the moment, Kid preferred Sticks and Leathe. The

mountains were what a fighter needed to be in his element. That was what went wrong with that stripper from Atlantic City. She did not understand the mountains, only the ocean. Her thing was the ocean, and that's all right. Everything in its time and place. But he was a mountain person, at least as long as he was a fighter he preferred the mountains to the ocean. When he retired, he'd get a condo in Atlantic City. But he would always keep a room in Sticks. He could never be away from the mountains for too long.

9.

His sisters were drinking and getting loud. They danced around Tony Bones to a Madonna song called "Music." Tony got annoyed. He pushed them away.

—Knock it off, he said.

They went back to drinking beer and whiskey and eating birthday cake from Carvel's. They had rented the room until five o'clock, and it was only twelve minutes after three.

The music stopped and the girls sat around the table. Now they were talking about old boyfriends. They discussed local boys they had crushes on. Then they discussed the cutest male cousins. Each sister had a different cousin she had a crush on. As they spoke with each other, their voices blurred. It created one big voice that Kid couldn't understand. It was just like when they were kids. They would sit around the dining room table. (This was before

Mr. Patterson took Kid upstate to get help with his temper and getting in trouble and skipping school and fighting.) They were crowded together. There were at least eleven of them. But the number could go as high as eighteen people if all of them visited home.

Nearly everyone spoke at once. A few were silent. They were invisible. Kid's mind was blank.

It was still blank.

There probably was some damage in his head. Kid had lost some memory. But if he couldn't remember what he lost, did it matter? Who cared? He had a body of memory. They were not thoughts but pictures and feelings that were packed into his muscles and his spine.

When Kid was a boy, he remembered reading about a great Mexican fighter named Salvador Sanchez, who was going to become a doctor after he retired from boxing. But Sanchez was killed in a car accident. All of Mexico mourned him. Parnell still remembered how he felt when he learned that the great Salvador Sanchez had been killed in a car accident. Salvador Sanchez—the invincible Salvador the fighter—was dead. It broke Kid's heart in a million pieces even though the Mexican fighter had died years before Kid knew this fact. It was reading about him in that book which upset Parnell Coole.

He was not planning on a medical career unless it was as an orderly. He was good with a mop.

Kid had a slight thickness in his speech. It was barely noticeable. His voice was a little thin. He seemed to whisper more than he talked. There was the faintest lisp. Yet, ask his sisters, he was always like that. They would tease him as a child and call him Al Pacino or Michael Corleone because of the whisper. They would mock the lisp, talking like drag queens.

Every couple of months Billy Faherty made Kid see a neurologist in Duchess County. His cat-scans were good. He didn't have any reflexive damage. If anything, his reflexes were better now than when he was a young fighter. Kid never was fast on his feet. Billy said that Kid Coole had good twitch muscles. He was not a sprinter. He was a long-distance runner. Kid was a reflexive fighter. His speed was with the counter-punch. His speed was with deception, not outright bursts of it. He was tricky, hard to figure, never where you thought he might be. He slipped punches by a centimeter, and then he countered.

Their mother died alert. She was active until the end. Her age was listed as being in her nineties. She fell down a staircase while visiting one of Kid's sisters in Brooklyn. Mom had not been to Brooklyn in thirty years.

The old man had pugilistic dementia. Their father did not know anyone or anything.

When his father was still mentally well, he told Kid that everyone forgets things. They do not remember a name or a date. What mattered was if you couldn't remember what things were for. You couldn't tell the difference between a spoon and a jack hammer. Kid had no trouble in that department. He had never picked up a jack hammer and expected a glass of tea to be drunk from it. He never wiped his ass and tasted the chocolate on his fingers. He knew where he was and who he was. He just did not have many words in his head. He was blank in the word-department of his brain. But his body had memories, aching thoughts of what he had done with himself through all those fights and all that sparring leading up to the fights, all that vigorous training, all the roadwork and gym workouts, the endless hours of sleeping and sleeping some more.

Kid spoke with one of his older brothers about his memory. The brother told him not to worry.

—It's all right, his brother said.

His brother Mickey suggested that Kid take ginkgo. Mickey Mack told him to build a memory palace in his mind. He said that Italian missionaries did this in China after Marco Polo went there. The priests taught the emperor's children how to memorize Chinese characters.

10.

—I walk into the vestibule of the palace of memory and look in a closet. It is filled with old coats, hats, baseball gloves, golf clubs, sneakers, winter coats, rain slickers, and tennis rackets. It smells of mildew. I sit inside of it in the dark. Then I get up and walk into the other rooms of the palace of memory.

—In the living room I sit on the couch. My mother makes me a tomato and cheese sandwich on Jewish rye with Gulden's golden mustard. I taste the pepper and salt on the tomato. The tomato came from our neighbor's garden. It is a beefsteak tomato, red and juicy. The juice runs down my chin.

—I watch television.

—A baseball game is on. A player is hit by a ball as he runs from first to second base. He crawls to the base but is tagged out. I find the second baseman cruel. Years later when I am introduced to the second baseman I refuse to shake his hand.—

11.

—Remember the Bee Gees? Oona asked.

They did. Who could forget the Bee Gees? The sisters let their recognition become known by screaming at the top of their lungs. His sisters were small but very loud creatures. They danced around the table again.

Sam shouted,

—Dancing at Lughnasa!—

Everyone laughed at this remark.

The music they danced to was by The Coors.

—Women, Tony Bones said. Then he added: Irish women are all nuts. But they're beautiful.

He shrugged his shoulders and lit a cigar and drank Scotch from a tumbler. The ice chinked on the side of the glass.

Kid tried to return to the palace of memory.

It occurred to him as he sat in a conference room of the Ramada Inn that he was twenty-six years old. He was getting to be a very old fighter. He needed more rooms in the palace of memory before he forgot everything. When his older brother told him to do this—to create the memory palace in his mind, not his body—he first thought about an old funhouse at Coney Island. He imagined Steeplechase or Luna Park. These were places that were there long before he was born. Kid never knew them. But his aunts and uncles and older cousins, plus his three oldest brothers, talked about these palaces of fun. His trainer Billy Faherty spoke about Steeplechase, and Mike White, his cutman, told him about Luna Park. The old-old fighters would tell him, when he met them at fight-writer dinners in Times Square, that they had their early career fights at the Coney Island Velodrome, and they fought there the same way Billy and Mike let him fight in Troy and Rome and Syracuse, building up a record for the big fights in Atlantic City, Las Vegas, or New York.

12.

The palace of memory was more a house than a castle. As much as Kid tried to make it grand, it kept coming back to a simple house. This house resembled the one they were raised in on Long Island. It had a cream-colored stucco exterior with green trim. Outside the front windows there was hollyhock growing. A lilac bush scented the yard. There was a great sycamore on the side of the house. But he couldn't see the house in his mind. His mind was like a white sheet hanging on a line to dry. The mind was full of nothingness. Where he saw the memory palace was in his muscles and bones, the ligaments and the guts of his body, in the pit of his stomach, through his kidneys on his backside, down the arcing and curling muscles of his legs, the thighs and quads, the kneecaps and the calves. He didn't really see the memory palace at all, though. He felt it inside of him, and he wondered whether he got his brother's instructions all wrong.

The house was worn out from all the children who lived in it. Its floors were scuffed and worn smooth from thousands of feet wearing away the polyurethane and then the wood itself. Many of the windows were cracked or had missing panes.

His palace of memory was drafty. Its kitchen was musty and small. The rooms were damp. Lighting was poor, sometimes only a bare light bulb in the middle of the ceiling. There were not too many rooms and only one bathroom, on the second floor. The one bathroom accommodated eighteen people.

Kid saw an uncle sleeping on the couch of memory. The uncle smelt of stale whiskey and tobacco. His trousers and socks were still on, but his jacket and shirt were draped over a chair in the living room. The snoring was loud and slow.

—Your brother has to go, his father said to their mother.

—He's a good kid, mom said. He's having a hard time.

—Aren't we all having a hard time, their father responded.

—He'll be back on his feet in no time, mom observed.

13.

His sisters listen as Deirdre talked about living in Brazil with her husband and daughters. When a sister asked what her husband did, Deirdre said,

—He works—

She had not learned to speak Portuguese, and that was a problem because her daughters spoke it now.

All of Kid's sisters were talking at once again. He couldn't understand a thing they were saying.

But Eileen was quiet like he was. Her nickname was Mouse. She used to be a nun. Now she worked for a wiseguy downtown, making his espressos for him.

Mary Grace filled their ears with obscenities.

—So I said to this fuckn motherfuckn shitass dirtbag, I says, hey, motherfuck, you listen to what I'm fuckn sayn.—

When Oona suggested that her sister watch her mouth, Mary Grace said,

—Hey, where I live in Brooklyn, even the fuckn priests talk like me.—

Tony Bones laughed.

—She ain't fuckn kiddin', he said.

14.

The manager of the Ramada Inn came in and reminded everyone to be out by five o'clock. Tony Bones put his arm on the manager's shoulder and the man became very apologetic about disturbing the party once Tony had talked to him.

—I straightened him out.—

Tony Bones winked at Kid Coole.

He came over to the fighter in the family.

—Where's ya fuckn brothers, Kid?—

Kid shrugged his shoulders as if to say, I don't know.

—What do you know, Kid?—

Kid shrugged again.

Tony punched him hard. His punch was a straight right. It landed on Kid's shoulder and it hurt. Tony was a big, muscular man. He laughed. He leaned over, being much taller than Kid Coole, and he planted a kiss on the top of Kid's shaved head. Then he stood behind Kid and Tony Bones kneaded his shoulders the way Mike White did before a fight.

—You're all right, Tony said. You mind your own fuckn business. You don't yap-yap like the rest your family. You seem more guinea than mick. I want you to meet a friend of mine in Brooklyn. He could help the management side of your career. Let Billy Faherty handle what he knows, the training of a fighter. Let my friend do what he knows best. Professional management. He'll create a financial future for you after you leave the ring. We'll put icing on your cake. I can make this champeenship fight happen at the Garden if you tell me to do it. But you got to let us manage you instead of Billy Farts. He'll stay your trainer. Otherwise you're gonna be fightn smokers in fuckn upstate for the rest of your career, Kid.

Mary Grace came over and collapsed into Tony's arms. She was drunk.

—Is my fiancé giving you a hard time? she asked Kid.

—I was telling him about a management opportunity, Tony said.

—The Kid won't remember a thing you tell him when he wakes up tomorrow. Am I right, bro'?—

Kid nodded his head yes.

To Tony he said,

—Speak to your guys. I'll tell Billy Faherty what's going on.—

Tony Bones stuck the cigar into his mouth, making him look like Al Capone, especially as he kept a fedora on his head, even inside the Ramada Inn. He pointed both of his thumbs skyward and waggled them.

—O.K., O.K., he said, shaking Kid's hand.

But Kid pulled his hand away almost immediately. Tony had an iron grip.

—How's my fuckn fiancé? Mary Grace asked.

—O.K., O.K., Tony said, letting her sit on his lap.

Mary Grace pulled the cigar out of his mouth and puffed on it, and Tony said she was crazy. Parnell Coole drifted away from them and decided it was time to go home. Everyone was drunk, and he didn't think any of his brothers were going to show. But just as he got to the door, Emmett and a bunch of the other brothers came in the door, so Kid put down his coat and stayed with his family a little longer.

1.

—Did you get a robe? Billy asks.

    —No, the Kid says, I don't need a robe.

—Robe's gonna make you look like a champeen.—

—I don't need a fuckn robe, Kid answers Billy Faherty.

The Kid grabs a long white towel and rips a hole in the center of it big enough to put his head through and for the ends to cover his chest, shoulders, and back.

—There's my robe, the fighter tells his trainer.

Billy Farts turns to Mike White.

—He's ready.—

Billy takes out a pair of boxing trunks from a plastic bag—green trunks with a yellow stripe on the seams and a gold shamrock on the front of them.

—What do you think? he asks.

—They suck, the Kid tells him. I hate all that phony shit.

—Easy does it, Billy Faherty says.

—You and your fuckn slogans.—

—Him and his fashions, Mike White says to Kid and nods in the direction of the trainer.

Billy Faherty wears a cheap purple and red nylon gym suit and old two-tone black-and-white sneakers. He's got a white terry cloth towel around his neck, and he hasn't shaved for several days.

The Kid picks up the Irish trunks and tosses them on

the floor. In their place he selects from his gym bag black nylon trunks with a white stripe down the seams.

—Okay, okay, Billy Faherty says. I was trying to add a classic touch, but I can see you aren't interested.

—I'm not interested, the Kid tells him.

Mike White lays out the other gear, including a protective cup, CoolMax socks so the Kid won't blister as his feet sweat from moving around the ring. Kid has a fairly new pair of high, black boxing shoes (—leather soft as a baby's ass, Billy Farts says.). There is also tape, scissors, ice, cotton swabs, water, Endswell, bucket, and liquid adrenaline for cuts.

Many of these things Mike White stuffs into pockets of his jacket. The jacket is blue and looks like something a surgeon might wear. But it is really a barber's jacket he brought from a friend in Leathe who has a haircut emporium there.

Mike White's daughter Penny White Half-Dog is their spit-bucket lady. But she won't come into the dressing room until the Kid is dressed and taped and almost ready to go.

In all the talk about Irish trunks Mike White has not said a word. He could care less about shamrock trunks. Mike White thinks Kid Coole is a pint-sized version of Joe Louis. He says the Kid—hey, Keed—fights like the old black fighters.

—Kid don't have an ounce of Irish in his fighting style, Mike White says.

People think Kid's Puerto Rican or Dominican or Cuban. They think he's Italian. Some think he's Jewish. Get him a white or yellow star or a star of David or trunks the color of the Italian flag. He's not wearing a goddamn gold shamrock on his trunks.

There is a knock at the door, and an assistant state commissioner enters, along with Lutrec Spears' trainer. Kid gives them both a dirty look.

—Who's taping my hands?—

Both Billy Faherty and Mike White tape his hands beautifully. But it is a matter of protocol in a championship fight. Billy is the trainer; Mike is the cutman. The trainer should tape the hands, and he does.

Lutrec Spears' trainer watches the taping along with an assistant state commissioner.

Taped hands make you feel powerful. Especially when Billy or Mike does it. When the Kid's sparring or working in the gym, he often tapes his own hands. But he needs a perfect taping now, so Billy will do the honors.

As Billy tapes the Kid's hands, Spears' trainer, Eddie Piano, objects.

—Make them looser, he says.

—It's not your fuckn business to see them tight or loose, Billy Faherty tells the opponent's trainer. Ask the commissioner you don't believe me.

—The tape is fine, the assistant commissioner says, and he then signs the taped hands with a permanent black marking pen.

—So don't break my balls, Billy says to Eddie.

They are old friends. But this is boxing, and they have a championship fight. The protocol is to make each other as uncomfortable as possible. The Kid and Mike White ignore both of them.

Eddie says,

—I'll break your fuckn head, Farty, you thick-headed donkey.—

After the hands are taped, Billy leaves with the assistant commissioner and Eddie Piano for Lutrec Spears' taping in his locker room.

The Kid has time to kill.

Now that he is taped and wearing his jockstrap and cup and black trunks and the boxing shoes and white socks Penny White Half-Dog joins her father Mike White to wait until the big moment.

Kid does situps on the massage table. He stretches. He walks back and forth. He shadow-boxes. But it is too early to break a sweat. Kid's just loosening up his muscles.

—You be fine, Penny says.

Kid smiles at her. It is the first time he's smiled all week. Everything has annoyed him lately. Everyone pisses him off.

Penny looks enormous in her bib overalls. Her hair is done up in corn-rows with bright-colored ribbons in her hair. All of this is for the Kid to see her—to be able to get back to the corner quickly and easily.

Ralph Half-Dog, the former spit-bucket man and Penny's beau, was still recuperating from his stroke, and he would not be in the arena.

2.

The Kid lies down on the rubbing table. He closes his eyes and tries to meditate. He lets his mind go blank.

Then he sits up. He gets up. He walks around. He paces. This is his first main event. It is also his first time fighting at Madison Square Garden. He's been an upstate fighter, a New York State Thruway fighter, going from Sticks to Leathe, Catskill to Troy, Schenectady to Rome, Utica to Syracuse and beyond. Just walking through the fighters' entrance on Thirty-third Street sent his normal pulse racing. Usually it is around 45 beats per minute. There it was more like 100 beats a minute. Now he has to control his emotions, channel them into one thing, to fight and beat his opponent (fuckn Spears) and win the championship.

—Lousy dressing room, the Kid says, looking around. You'd think the Garden would give you a deluxe place.

—It ain't half bad, Mike White says.

—I seen uglier, Penny agrees.

Billy is still in the other guy's dressing room breaking chops over the taping.

The Kid goes off to a corner and jumps rope.

—Don't get too worked up, Mike White says.

—Don't worry about me, Kid says. Worry about what your job is.

—You are my job, Mike says.

—Worry about how much ice and water you got in the fuckn bucket. Worry about the Endswell. Worry about the cotton swabs.—

Billy Farts walks back in.

—Fuckn bastards, he says.

—What? Mike asks.

—That fuckn Eddie Piano's breaking my balls again.—

—What else is new, Billy?—

Then Billy Faherty looks at the Kid.

—You ain't sweatin'.—

The Kid does some sit-ups. He jumps rope. He jogs in place. He shadow-boxes. He's sweating now.

At around ten o'clock a man from the Garden comes in and says,

—Half hour to show time. Be up and ready. Get your fighter warmed up—

Warmed up? The Kid's dripping with sweat. He's ready. He's on fire. Let's go.

Now he's pacing back and forth. He wants to go out and fight. Enough of this preparation. Enough of the media. Enough of commissioners and assistant commissioners and Garden officials and corporate sponsors. Enough of teachers in high school. Enough of people who never believed in him. Enough of those who wanted the worst for him. Enough of the ones who thought him a complete nobody. To hell with his family, his mother and father, his brothers and sisters. His aunts and uncles, cousins and grandparents, great uncles and great aunts. To hell with them all. He's fighting for the lightweight championship, and he's here, and they are not. They are there.

—I'm here, Kid says.

—Course you here, sugar, Penny Half-Dog says. Where else you be but here?

—I'm fuckn here.—

Penny just smiles at him now. She knows all about fighters. Their brains are not like other people's brains. They have funny ways of thinking and expressing themselves. God bless them all, she thinks. I'm just the spit-bucket lady. But him, the Kid, he has a beef. Its name is Lutrec Spears. He's the beef. Kid has a grudge against him.

At the weigh-in the day before, downtown across from City Hall, he called the Kid

—a jew bastard—

—I'm not Jewish, Kid said.

—Quit the jawin', Billy Faherty warned him. Settle with him in the ring.

—Jew bastard, Lutrec shouted.

Lutrec had become a Moslem.

Now the Kid's a jew bastard.

—Ready, the man from the Garden yells into their quarters.

3.

The Kid wears eight-ounce gloves. Red ones. Reyes. Mike has Kid's mouthpiece in the bucket.

Parnell "Kid" Coole jukes down the aisle toward the lighted ring. A medley of music plays. He picked it himself. James Brown (—don't want nobody open the door I'll get it myself—). House of Pain. Van Morrison. One bleeding into the other.

He runs up the steps to the ring and steps quickly through the ropes and bounces around the ring in his black leather boxing shoes. The canvas under his feet feels good. He circles the ring. He throws punches and nods to people in the front row. He says hello to Tony Bones in the front row. Tony takes one of his thumbs and points it skyward, and then waggles it. Kid winks to him. Tony smiles.

Where's Lutrec Spears?

He comes down the aisle to the music of Bob Marley and then some French music. He runs up the steps and steps into the ring. They applaud him wildly. He wears a black cape which flies in the air as he dances around the ring.

They nearly collide.

The ref tells them to go to their corners.

Mike White rubs the Kid's back muscles, getting him limber.

—Are you ready? Mike White asks.

—I'm ready.—

—Ready? Penny Half-Dog asks.

—Ready.—

—Are you ready, Kid? Billy Faherty asks him.

—Yeah, I'm ready, he says.

—Then let's go, Billy says.

The Kid dances side to side to side to side, all around the ring. The ref tells him to stay on his side of the ring until the Kid is told to come out. But the Kid ignores him. As soon as the ref isn't looking the Kid inches back around the ring.

He doesn't look at Lutrec except out of the corner of

his eye. Lutrec looks good. Kid'll give him that. He looks real good. He's big for a lightweight, much taller than Kid Coole. His reach is a few inches longer. His legs look six inches longer than the Kid's. But none of this bothers the Kid. He's ready to fight Lutrec Spears.

When the referee brings them to the center of the ring to give them the instructions, Kid looks directly at Lutrec Spears for the first time. Lutrec's staring at him in this tough-guy way. The opponent—the other guy—is just staring. Kid's no tough guy. He's just tough enough. He's blank like a combat soldier who's going out to hump the boonies looking for the enemy. This is the other guy. The opponent. It's nothing personal. They are going to fight. Whoever wins will be the new lightweight champion of the world.

Tough enough, Kid says to himself.

They go to their corners.

The bell rings.

Kid trots out. Lutrec runs across the ring.

Kid slips Spears' first punch and counters with one of his own which Spears slips. Lutrec throws a huge right that Kid slips, and Lutrec's momentum carries him over to the piling in the neutral corner where Kid races to bash him in the head.

Lutrec Spears wheels around. He throws quick jabs followed by real punches. Right. Left. Uppercut.

The uppercut misses the Kid's jaw by a quarter of an inch. Had it landed, the Kid would be counted out. Kid had been off balance.

Lutrec's cute. That's how Billy Faherty would phrase it.

—Real cute.—

Awkward.

He's fast, for one thing. Very reflexive. He's never where you think he's going to be. His punches don't look like much. But when they land, they hurt.

The Kid's opponent is very loose and flexible. Kind of rubbery almost. He's like Michael Spinks when the younger of the Spinks brothers was the light-heavyweight champion. He slips the Kid's punches. He doesn't have bones in his body from the way he pivots and bends to slip a punch.

The Kid has yet to land a good one.

Kid's stance is flat-footed. His brain seems drugged.

Lutrec Spears misses several punches. He lands the jab. But when he follows with a big punch, Kid slips it.

Missing is very painful. It pulls your back muscles apart. Your back can go into spasms.

Finally Kid Coole hits Lutrec Spears solid on the jaw off a counterpunch the Kid threw coming under the jab.

Lutrec Spears is able to take a punch.

He says something in French to Kid Coole.

—*Merde*, he says.

Lutrec sticks out his face to show that Kid Coole's punch has no effect. But the Kid has his attention.

The bell rings to end the first round.

4.

Kid turns to find the corner. Where is Ralph Half-Dog? Then he remembers. Ralph had a stroke. Kid sees Ralph's wife Penny waving him into the corner and the stool. Then Kid sees Mike White. Next he sees Billy Farts.

One minute goes by quickly. His pulse goes from 180 beats per minute down to 50. They work frantically on what it is they have to do.

Billy does not look pleased.

—That was too close to call, he says. You need to come out strong the last minute in the round, Kid.

The bell rings.

Kid is not even off his stool.

5.

Lutrec Spears is in his face. He lands a punch on the Kid's stomach. He follows it with one to the ear. Kid spins and gets out of the corner. The Kid moves around the ring.

As Spears pursues him, Kid plants his feet, and he lands a left to the opponent's liver which stuns him.

Kid's knocked out people with that punch. But Lutrec Spears comes on stronger after the Kid popped him one.

Kid dances around the ring.

6.

Lutrec Spears won Round One by coming on with flash at the end of the round. But Kid Coole wins Round Two with a jab. The jab is the best it's ever been. It has snap. Menace. Power. The Kid senses the sting at the end of it, like it's a scorpion's tail. In Round Three, Spears showboats. There is nothing fancy in the Kid's own style. He's paired it down to essence. It's elemental. He jabs. He moves. He jabs. He sets. He lands a punch. He steps away. He dances left. He jabs again. Nothing fancy. Kid's economical. He's elementary. Fundamental.

Lutrec Spears has got something like a bolo punch. He throws it from the hip. It is a right cross that hooks in. But it comes as an uppercut. Kid's never seen anything like it nor has he felt anything like it when it grazes his lower chin or hits his Adam's apple.

Kid Coole has a welt under his eye from a left hook, then a follow up with the bolo from the right as he tries to slip a faked jab.

7.

Mike White gets the swelling down in the one-minute rest between the rounds.

The bell rings.

Kid goes across the ring towards the other guy, his opponent.

Lutrec Spears fights in flourishes. Kid goes three minutes every round. He paces himself. Lutrec goes in spurts, then he comes on at the end of the round.

At the end of the round, Billy Faherty kneels in front of Kid Coole as Mike White works on the swelling and his daughter Penny hands him his tools.

—How am I doing? Kid asks.

—He's taking rounds from you, Billy says. You need to step it up at the end of the round, Kid.

—Okay, Kid says.

—The jab is a thing of beauty, says Billy.

—It's the best jab I ever had.—

—Focus, Billy says. No words. No thoughts. Actions. Reflexes. Act and react. Jab and move. Punch and counterpunch. Whack him!

The bell rings.

Kid trots to center-ring.

They get it on.

8.

Lutrec Spears is very fast. Kid needs to time his counterpunch just right if he wants to slow his opponent down. But the Kid is beating him to the punch. Kid notices that Lutrec feints when the Kid fakes the jab. That's because the jab is working.

The jab won't open a cut.

But a good jab will allow another punch to open a cut

later. The jab makes Lutrec's face swell. Once it swells enough, the Kid'll slice it open with a hook or cross or head-butt (accidentally, of course). Uppercut. The tape on the gloves nicking his face.

Spears flinches when the Kid lands the jab. He pulls back. Kid is taking him out of his rhythm. If Lutrec Spears pulls back, he can't throw the bolo. He's not within range to land it or his hook or the straight right, though Kid Coole is beginning to understand that Lutrec Spears does not have a straight right, only that cork-screwing uppercut-right cross. His bolo.

The bolo hooks in from down below around his waist.

When it lands, Kid hurts. Spears has the biggest punch the Kid's ever encountered. It hurts all over when he lands it well. Kid dances away, wincing.

9.

The other guy fights in outbursts. A series of ten fast punches in combination. Then he drifts through a round. He floats. Then he repeats the flourish at the end of the round.

Kid manages to punch the opponent good in his hip joints on both sides of his body without the referee warning or taking away a point. The punches slow down Lutrec's gliding side-stepping and put him more squarely in front of Kid Coole.

Lutrec Spears throws a bolo.

It lands on the tip of Kid's nose, and it stings.

Kid dances away.

Spears pursues him.

Kid's legs are good. He has a lot of stamina. His punches get stronger as the fight progresses. He is not a knockout artist. The punches accumulate. The combination of the punches turns into one big hurt.

By Round Eight it adds up to a throbbing pain in the other guy's system.

But Kid's never gone twelve rounds other than in a gym brawl or sparring session.

Who owns Round Eleven? Who Twelve?

That's who wins.

Neither Lutrec Spears nor Kid Coole is a knockout fighter. They're boxers. Little guys. Lightweights. Kid's an old-fashioned, no-nonsense fighter. Lutrec's a dazzling hummingbird of a fighter.

The bell rings to end Round Nine.

10.

Kid turns to look for his corner. Where's Ralph Half-Dog? There is no Ralphie anywhere. Big fat Ralph Half-Dog in his bib overalls and his black hair in long Indian braids. That's right. He's sick. He had a stroke. He's home in bed, watching the match on the cable television.

Then Kid sees Ralph's big wife Penny in bib overalls and her hair in corn-rows waving him to the corner.

Kid sits on the wooden stool. His breath is short. It is hard to focus. His ribs hurt. His chest aches with each breath. His head feels foggy and swollen. His arms ache like he had flu. His legs are getting tired.

—Where's the bolo? Billy Faherty asks.

The Kid is not sure what he means.

Mike White drops a bunch of ice down the Kid's trunks and sticks smelling salts under his nose.

Kid jumps. He screams.

Billy slaps the Kid hard in the face. He holds the fighter's face in his rubber-gloved hands to get his attention.

—The bolo is conspicuous by its absence, Billy Farts says.

Kid doesn't understand what it is the old trainer is saying.

—You're getting to him. Keep doin' what you're doin'. Jab. Move. Jab. Set. Whack him good! Whack this motherfucker hard, Kid. Then move again.—

11.

The stool is pulled out of the ring.

Bell rings.

Kid trots to the center of the ring.

Dance left. Right. Jab. Move. Jab. Set. Unload a hook. Land it hard on his liver. Get out of there!

By Round Eleven, they fight on the inside. They are no longer moving around. The Kid takes blows. Lutrec Spears takes them, too. This is the Kid's kind of fight. This is the kind of match he likes. He's an inside kind of guy. Kid likes to go toe to toe with the opposition. (Most of the time Billy Faherty won't let him go toe to toe, but Kid likes mixing it up this way.) He enjoys the other guy's breath so close to his face. It's intimate. Personal. It's the way he wins.

Lutrec's combinations are crisp again. He's back to the flourishes in the beginning, middle, and end of the round.

Kid wounds him with a straight right that bursts inside the other guy's nose. Blood gushes out. Wounded, Spears fights better. Kid takes a big hook to the ear that rocks him back on his heels. The Kid loses his balance. The would-be champion pursues the challenger.

They clinch.

Ref breaks them apart. Makes them come to the center. They clinch again. Ref breaks them again.

Their legs move in a slow motion around the ring.

Lutrec Spears' punches are bigger than ever.

The punches hurt so much the Kid could cry. But the adrenaline deadens the pain. Kid fights on. So does Lutrec Spears. The opponent fights through his own pain.

The distance between them keeps halving. They are fighting the Kid's kind of fight. The arcs get smaller and smaller. Their legs don't even move. They stand in the center of the ring exchanging blows. Kid is on the inside, landing short, painful blows to Spears in rapid succession. The other guy obliges Parnell Kid Coole with the same.

This is what it is all about.

Lutrec's punches land. They hurt. But they are not

271

cleanly thrown. So they do not land cleanly. Kid's own punches are sharper. They land more solidly. There is no hollow ring when they land on Lutrec's body. They have a thud to them.

If Kid were fighting anyone else, he would have had a K.O. His punches are tight and good. They land heavily on the face and raise lumps all over the body.

12.

Round Twelve: Kid fights his own fight. He doesn't waste anything. Not even an extra breath. Everything is economical about his style. He jabs. Then he abandons the jab and goes inside. He bangs the body on both sides. Liver one side. Spleen the other.

When Spears scores on him, Kid clinches.

Ref breaks them apart.

Kid doesn't hesitate now.

Jab isn't going to do anything at this point in a fight.

Kid keeps banging away at the body. Then the Kid gives Lutrec a good uppercut that brushes his jawline. Then the Kid hooks over Lutrec's shoulder and cuffs the champ's ear. Kid follows this with a straight right. It lands. Right on Lutrec's cheekbone. It is not a knockout punch. But Kid stuns Lutrec.

By the end, Lutrec Spears has no more flourishes left in him.

The bell rings.

People flood the ring as Lutrec stumbles to his corner.

Kid pivots and looks for Ralph Half-Dog who is not there anymore. Sick. Stroke. In bed. Home. But not his wife.

He sees Penny White Half-Dog running toward him with her hair in corn-rows and in her bib overalls with her big arms opened wide. She pulls Kid Coole into her enormous bosom and swallows him into her arms. She is probably twice the fighter's size.

—This is your fight, Kid, she says, kissing him all over the bumps on his face.

Mike White, her father, runs over to his fighter.

—You did good, he says, hugging the Kid hard. You was great, Kid.

—What a tough bastard! The Kid shouts to Billy Faherty who embraces his fighter and kisses both of the Kid's cheeks as he holds the beat-up face in his own big old swollen hands.

Mike White drips cold water from the sponge over the Kid's head. Then he makes the Kid put the towel with the slit in the middle of it over his head.

—I love you, Kid, Billy says.

Billy Farts is crying.

Kid says that he loves Billy, too. The fighter puts his arms around the trainer, and he cries, too.

Mike White throws a big new white terry cloth towel over the Kid's head and wraps another one over his shoulders so he doesn't get cold.

—You were great, Billy Farts says. That was the best fight I ever saw, Kid.

They wait for the judges' decision.

13.

Two judges score it five-five-two for each of them. Lutrec Spears wins five rounds. The Kid wins five. They each split two. The deciding judge is Tippy Cohen-Levine, a man from Albany. He scores it seven-five.

The Kid looks at Billy. Kid looks at Mike. He looks at Penny.

Across the ring, Lutrec Spears can't get off his stool to wave to the crowd. They administer salts to him. A doctor checks his eyes, shining a light in them to see if he gets any response.

Lutrec Spears is the lightweight champion of the world.

The Kid looks at his corner again. They look back at Kid Coole.

The ring fills with more people. They shout. They shove each other around.

An announcer sticks a microphone under the Kid's nose.

—How does it feel? he asks him.

Billy Faherty shoves the microphone away from the Kid's face.

—This is a travesty! he says. Kid Coole won that fight!

Announcer sticks the microphone in the Kid's face again.

—How do you feel, Kid?—

Penny White Half-Dog jumps in the announcer's face and grabs the microphone from him.

—How you think he feels? she asks. That's a dumb-ass question. He feels like shit. Empty. Robbed. That's how he feel. He feel robbed. You ever been robbed? That's what it feel like. It feel like robbed.

Billy and Mike tug the Kid away as Penny keeps jawing with the announcer.

Mike takes off the gloves. He secures the towel with the hole in the middle of it with the other towels around the waist and he wraps new towels around Kid Coole's head. He slides a bag of ice around the Kid's face to counter the swelling on the right cheek.

Lutrec Spears is helped from the ring and put on a stretcher and taken away.

The Kid goes down the aisle and out of the arena and into the locker room where his clothes and valuables are stored. He showers and gets dressed and meets the corner-people outside on Thirty-third.

They walk to a parking lot two blocks from the Garden.

The Kid gets in the back of the van with Penny.

Mike White drives the van up the West Side Highway, catches the Taconic in Westchester, and heads north toward home. As he drives the Kid calculates what he earned. After expenses, fees to his corner, and taxes, he will take home a check for ten-thousand dollars. The original check was two-hundred-fifty-thousand dollars.

Billy Faherty, being an alcoholic in recovery, likes to say,
—Easy does it.—

But it's really easy come, easy go.

Billy talks to Mike about the old days. He mentions Rocky and Cus and Gus and Jimmy and Billy and Joe and Henry and Lou and Barney and Benny and Archie and, of course, Ali and Sonny. Ali and Joe. Ali and George. Ali versus Ken. Ali versus Leon. Ali versus Larry.

Penny Half-Dog leans over and touches Kid Coole's sore face.

—You won, she says.

Then to her father, Mike White, who is driving, she says,

—Coole here won that damn fight, Daddy.—

—Of course, Coole won, sugar, Mike White says. Kid Coole won.

—He won, Billy Farts says, and Lutrec Spears is lightweight champion.

—Maybe I didn't fight hard enough, the Kid tells them. Billy says,

—You won.—

As they drive north upstate and into the night, Billy Faherty says,

—Take some time off.—

The Kid already knew what Billy wanted him to do which was to stop fighting and do something else.

—Decide what you want to do, Billy Faherty says. After you've given it some thought.

Billy doesn't want to train him anymore, the Kid figured. He wants this to be his last fight.

—Maybe I didn't fight hard enough, the Kid repeats.

—You won the fuckn fight, Mike White says.

—Yeah, that's right, Penny White Half-Dog tells the Kid. You fuckn won that fight all right, man.

—He won the fuckn fight, Billy Farts says.

M. G. Stephens (Michael Gregory Stephens) was born in Washington, D.C., and grew up in Bedford-Stuyvesant, Brooklyn, and further out on Long Island, into a family of sixteen children. His father came from Ireland and his mother was from an old New England family whose ancestors included a North African indentured servant to the Wheelock family, the founders of Dartmouth College. His mother grew up in a 27-room Brooklyn mansion on Madison near Stuyvesant, right where Spike Lee shot *Do the Right Thing*, which was also a few blocks from where Stephens lived as a child. He has been around boxing all his life. He also worked various jobs, including a stint in the Merchant Marine, greens-keeping, being a caddy, Christmas tree salesman on the Lower East Side, gas-pump jockey, dishwasher, East Asia correspondent, bartender, and of course journeyman boxer and sparring partner. He lived for many years (15) in London, but now resides just north of Chicago, and has been exiled from New York for over twenty-five years. *Kid Coole* is the third novel about the Coole family, the other two being *The Brooklyn Book of the Dead* and *Season at Coole*, whose fiftieth anniversary of its publication by E. P. Dutton is in 2022. These novels comprise *The Coole Trilogy*. Besides *Kid Coole*, Spuyten Duyvil has just published Stephens' novel, *King Ezra*, about Ezra Pound.

Made in United States
North Haven, CT
25 June 2024

54042234R00168